A New Hero

The Adventures of Silver Dove, Book Thirteen

Eliza Scalia

ISBN 978-1-965352-41-0

DEDICATION

Dedicated to Sonja Dalton, a woman who has shown me endless support for anything I set my mind to. She has done more for me than I could ever say.

Chapter One

Colomba-
A New
Beginning

The end of summer sunshine comes through the windows of the diner, but I cannot feel it because of the strong air conditioning. That's something I am truly grateful for, since I still feel the sweat on me from walking over here almost thirty minutes ago. Luis and I are sitting across the table from Nat and her girlfriend Kaley. The four of us have been having a great time together just chatting about everything that has happened this summer. Sadly, tomorrow this summer break is coming to an end, and we have to go to school again. We are all upset about this, but we also recognize that we are excited to start this year since we will be seniors. This is our last year of school together before we are pretty much adults.

There is a lot to look forward to this year. I mean, at the end of last year Luis finally figured out that we are Silver Dove and the Crow. Over the summer we have started training together as well as using our powers to help out whenever we could. It took a while for all the people in town to get used to him no longer being the bad guy, but they are starting to trust him now. I've had a really great time with him. I can only hope that this continues as the school year starts.

As Luis tells us about a movie he saw the other night, I look into his eyes, feeling very confused. I think back to what my grandma said about Luis and I. She said that those who have the medals are destined to end up together. When I look at Luis though, I don't really know what to feel.

Luis has been one of my best friends for years, I don't know if I could ever think of him as a boyfriend. I mean he was even my enemy for the longest time as the Crow, how can we ever be more than just friends? He is an incredibly sweet guy, he is very creative, he's a good friend, and he's also pretty smart. Any girl would be lucky to have him as a boyfriend. I just don't know if I'm that girl though. I don't even know if he cares about me that way. He has helped me out so much since I have met him, and has always been there for me, but that might have just been him being a good friend. He even got Alex to stop bugging me at the junior prom last year.

He probably doesn't feel that way about me, we've known each other so long, if he did care about me like that then he would have said something by now. When I look at him though, I can't help but wonder what it would be like to be with him. I can't help but think about how wonderful it could be, but that might just be a something that could never happen, it could just be a dream.

Chapter Two

Luis-
A New Hope

Beside me, Colomba laughs as I tell them a story, and I am stunned by how beautiful she is no matter what. As I look at her, I can't believe how lucky I am. When Shadow first told me that the people who share the medals are supposed to be together, I was not happy about it. I knew that I love Colomba, and it seemed like a mistake that I would end up with Silver Dove. I hated Silver Dove then and it felt like I was living my worst nightmare hearing Shadow say that I was destined to be with her. Now that I know that Silver Dove is Colomba, I feel as if I will never be upset again. How could I ever be upset knowing that I'm going to end up with the most perfect girl in the world?

I've loved her since the moment I met her almost three or four years ago. Alex and I used to fight over her, but I've won now. She and Alex don't even talk to each other anymore. I can never put into words how happy I am that that psycho is out of her life. I'm okay with him wrecking his own life, that's his choice, but I am glad that he's not going to drag her along with him.

When I look at her, I can't believe that everything has worked out so perfectly. After all the terrible things that have happened in my life, I finally have something truly wonderful happen. Even though we figured out who the other is at the end of last year, we haven't really talked to each other about that though. It's almost as if we are both too afraid to talk about how we are destined to be together. I guess it's because it would be super embarrassing and uncomfortable to talk about how we are going to be in love and get married and all that even though we are still in high school. As I look at her as she tells her own story, I can't help but think about how beautiful she would look in a wedding dress. She would be the most beautiful thing on earth, I just know it.

It's okay if we haven't talked about it yet though, we have time. We have our whole lives to talk about it. I love her, so I will be patient and wait until we are both comfortable with the idea. I mean, we are both still getting used to the idea that we are Silver Dove and the Crow. I'm sure that we will talk about it some time before this school year ends. We are both trying to get into the same college, but I would like to be able to tell her how I truly feel before that happens. We have a year until then, I'm sure we can figure it out.

For now, I am just happy to have her happy beside me, both of us honest with each other about who we really are. If she is happy, then I will always be happy.

Chapter Three

Colomba-
A New
Student

The day has just begun on the first day of school. Nat and I are in the library since I wanted to grab something, while Luis ran off to go speak to his favorite teacher, Mr. Sizemore the art teacher. Even though it was cray hot yesterday, it's a lot cooler today since it had rained all last night and a little bit this morning. My rain boots squeak from the moisture from the rain as I step on the top step of the little step stool so that I can look at the top shelf of books. I keep my eyes on the books as I speak to down Nat.

"What do you hope will happen this year Nat? I mean, we're seniors now, most people make big plans for themselves senior year." Nat just shrugs her shoulders.

"I want to survive this year. The year just started, and I'm already stressed. Everything just seems to be crashing in all at once." I nod my head at that as my eyes continue to scan over the book titles, trying to find something interesting.

"Yeah, I know what you mean." And I really do. Just this morning my dad was trying to talk to me about applying to colleges. Just the thought of that made the blueberry pancakes I was eating churn in my belly. I know that I've been wanting to go to college my entire life, but the thought of it still scares me. What really terrifies me about it is the thought that I may not get into any college that I want. Nat has been telling me all summer that I'm being silly, that any college would be happy to take me, but I'm still nervous about it. Sometimes it feels like I am the only one doubting myself.

"Hey, I'm going to be here a minute to find something I want, so you can go on ahead. I'll see you later." Nat walks off while I continue looking at the books. It is silent except for the occasional squeak from my boots on the stool. I notice that a small puddle has formed on the top step, but I notice it too late. My feet slip on the stool, and I feel myself fall backward. I close my eyes, expecting to hit the ground and feel a wave of pain run through me, I know I will be feeling any second. Every second that passes feels like an eternity, but the pain still doesn't come. Right when I feel like I should be hitting the ground, I feel something catch me in midair. What's going on? Whatever is holding me feels gentle and careful, what is this?

"Are you alright?" The voice is deep and calm, a soothing voice of a young man.

I open my eyes to see the most handsome young man I've ever seen holding me in his arms. His golden hair seems to glow in the dim light of the library. Even though he is a bit muscular and athletic looking, there is a gentleness about him that makes me instantly comfortable with him. His bright green eyes look deeply into mine with concern. When I see the concern in his eyes, I suddenly realize that I haven't answered his question.

"Oh yes, yes I'm fine." He smiles at me, and I feel my heart pounding in my chest.

"Good, I was worried about you." I feel my face grow warm when he says that he was worried about me. Something in his eyes tells me that he is telling the truth. Those brilliant green eyes look deeply into mine and it feels like I'm getting lost in those emerald eyes. He opens his mouth to reveal perfect white teeth as he speaks to me again.

"My name is Anthony Amarelli, what is yours?" I clear my throat, afraid that I will sound nervous.

"My name is Colomba, Colomba Carter." His eyes grow wide for a split second when he hears my first name. I don't know why he does this, but I don't let my mind stay on that thought for very long because he continues to speak to me.

"Colomba, that is a beautiful name." My heart is beating so fast that it almost feels like a bird is beating its wings as fast as it can so that it can fly in my chest.

"Thank you." I look away from his gaze for a moment in embarrassment. It is only at that moment that I realize that he is still holding me in his arms. "W- Would you mind setting me down?" He grins at me with complete confidence.

"Of course, my apologizes." He slowly and

steadily sets me down, back on my own two feet. I'm almost glad that he was holding me when I first saw him or else he might have noticed my knees wobbling in my nervousness.

"Are you sure that you are alright?" I smile, feeling so happy that he is concerned about me.

"Yes, I'm alright thanks to you." He smiles warmly at me, and it feels like I'm going to melt all over the floor.

"Well, I would like to make sure that you are fine so would you mind if I walked with you to your first class?" His smile is so warm and gentle that I don't even think before I give him my answer.

"I would like that." His smile broadens as the two of us leave the library. He walks close beside me, and I wish that he would get just a little bit closer. Anthony walks with a confident stride while I stare down at my feet, a little nervous about looking at him.

"A-are you new at this school? I don't think that I've ever seen you before." That is definitely true. This school is really small. I may not know everybody here personally, but I could probably recognize most people's faces here. But I have definitely never seen this guy before. This guy is so handsome that anybody would notice him.

"Yes, I just moved here to Drew's Hollow over the summer." He glances down at me with a smile. "I think that I'm going to like it here." I glance back down, feeling my cheeks grow warm.

"I hope that you do, Anthony."

"What do you enjoy doing, Colomba?"

"Well, I really like doing martial arts, reading,

and needlework like knitting and quilting."

"Martial arts? You seem like a very impressive young lady. Judging from how you carry yourself, I'm guessing that you are very good at it. There is just an aura of silent power about you. You seem very gentle and sweet, but you seem to have the power to defend yourself if necessary." I don't know how he sees that, but something about the way he said it lets me know that he's telling the truth. I can already feel my cheeks growing warm, and I know that I must be blushing like crazy.

"Thank you, that is very sweet of you to say. What kind of things are you interested in?" Anthony doesn't even take a second to think about it before he gives me an answer.

"I enjoy reading, archery, and boxing for the most part." He says this as if it means nothing even though those hobbies are pretty cool.

"Wow, archery and boxing sound really fun. I would love to learn how to do that one of these days." Anthony smiles down at me.

"Well, maybe I can show you some time. I think we can both have a great time with it." I look away from him again, a little too nervous to look in his eyes when I respond.

"I would like that a lot." My happiness suddenly changes to disappointment when I see where we are. "Oh, well here's my first class. I guess I will see you later?" I ask him, begging for him to say yes. He is smiling warmly at me, making me melt all over the floor again.

"Of course, I would be so happy to see you again." He gives me a simple wave and a wink before he turns around to head down the hall. I watch him leave for only a moment before I head into my first class as well. When I sit down, it takes me an entire minute to calm down my heart. Oh my gosh, I have never felt this way before. When I was with him, everything felt so perfect. It was as if nothing else in the world existed except for the two of us. It was so wonderful.

I don't get too much time to think about this though since the teacher starts our first class of the new year. I try to focus on what they are talking about, but my mind keeps going back to Anthony. Several more classes pass by just like this, sadly it doesn't seem that I share those classes with Anthony, but I have a few that I share with Nat and Luis. It isn't until lunch that I finally have that feeling of perfection come back to me.

I sit down at our usual table with Nat, Luis and Kaley haven't come out of the line yet with their food yet. As we start chatting about how our first day of school is going so far, Nat suddenly perks up as she looks at something across the cafeteria.

"Hey, check out the new guy!" Nat looks behind me with wide eyes. I turn around in my seat to see Anthony stepping out of the cafeteria line with his tray.

He glances around the room for a moment, and I can see many girls looking at him. I can tell from looking into their eyes that they're hoping that Anthony will sit with them, but he doesn't even pay attention to them. His eyes finally stop their search around the room when he sees me. He grins as he walks over to my table. Nat's eyes grow even wider when she sees this.

"Is he coming toward us? Do you know him?" I look away from my friend's curious eyes.

"Yeah, I met him this morning in the library after you left. I was falling off the stool and he caught me before I hit the ground. He's a really cool guy, his name is Anthony." When I look back up at Nat, her entire face is lit up with excitement.

"Oh my gosh! That sounds like something out of a romance novel! I'm so jealous!" I smile softly as I feel a blush forming on my cheeks.

"Don't let your girlfriend hear that Nat or you'll be in big trouble." She just smirks at me like I'm being ridiculous.

"Oh c'mon Birdy, any girl would be jealous of a meet cute like that." I look at her, confusion all over my face.

"Meet cute? What on earth is a meet cute?" Nat doesn't get to answer me since Anthony has arrived, standing in front of our table, smiling down at the both of us.

"Hello Miss Colomba." I look up at him, a smile instantly coming to my face.

"Hi Anthony. How are you?"

"I am doing well now that I'm here with you." He flashes me an amazing smile and I feel a shiver run down my spine. I can't believe that a guy this handsome and charming actually exists outside of the movies. "Would you mind if I sat with you two today?"

"Of course you can. Please sit." He sits down beside me, making my stomach do flips in my chest. Oh my gosh I am so nervous and so happy at the same time. I clear my throat to try not to sound too scared when I ask him, "How has your first day at Drew's Hollow High been going so far?" He looks around at the cafeteria where I can see so many people looking our way, mostly girls looking over at us with jealousy, wondering why he is sitting with us instead of them.

"It has gone well, I think. People here are very friendly." He smiles warmly at me. "I was a bit sad to see that you weren't in any of my classes this morning, but I am glad that we can at least have lunch together." From the corner of my eye, I can see Nat smiling at me slyly. She seems just as impressed as I am with how slick this guy is with his compliments. I am probably blushing so hard right now that my entire face most likely looks like a tomato.

"Wow Birdy, look at you already making friends on the first day. Look at you being popular." Nat says sarcastically, and I give her a little playful punch on the shoulder in response. Anthony looks at us curiously.

"What is this name that you just called her?" Anthony asks with confusion on his face. I laugh softly.

"Birdy, it's just a nickname that she's been calling me since we were kids." He smiles at me warmly.

"Well, your real name is so beautiful that I don't think I could ever call you anything else." I lower my gaze from his, feeling myself blush even more.

"Thank you, that's very sweet of you to say." He chuckles at me.

"I speak the truth. It seems as if everything about

you is beautiful." When she hears this Nat smiles so wide that it practically covers her face. It only lasts a moment before it disappears to be replaced by a look of discomfort, and even a little fear. I don't even have a chance to ask her what caused her to feel this way before I am given the answer.

"Hey there new guy, how you doin'?" I turn around to see Angela looking at Anthony like she is a hunter and he is her prey. Anthony looks at her though with a mixture of confusion and annoyance.

"I am fine, and who are you?" He asks, trying to be polite, but not able to completely hide his annoyance. She giggles at him in a way I have never heard her giggle. Whenever I've heard Angela laugh it's usually a mean cackle that she lets out whenever she's making fun of someone. This giggle though almost sounds girlish, like she's trying to flirt with him. Oh my gosh she is flirting with him, isn't she? I think I'm going to puke.

"Oh c'mon, don't be mean. You remember me from second period, don't you? I sit right behind you." She moves in closer to him, getting in between Anthony and me. I want to say something rude to her, but Anthony beats me to it.

"Do you have a reason for talking with me right now?" From his tone, I can easily see that his annoyance is quickly turning into anger. It's obvious though that Angela is really trying to ignore that fact as she keeps trying to flirt with him.

"Well, I was wondering why you are sitting over here with these two when you can come sit with me and my friends. You can meet a lot more interesting people there and we can show you all the fun stuff around town after school. With you being new and all, I thought you might appreciate that." Anthony narrows his green eyes when he hears the little insult she gave to Nat and I by saying that she and her friends are more interesting than us.

"I believe that I will be just fine here, thank you. I'm sure from what I have heard you talk about in our second period, that the conversation will be a lot more interesting over here." The glare he gives her after saying that sends a shiver down my spine. I can only imagine how Angela feels though with that glare directed right at her. She clears her throat awkwardly before she straightens herself up, trying to make her face look like she doesn't care about him rejecting her. I can see the pain in her eyes though. Angela is hurt that this cool, handsome guy chose to sit with me instead of her.

"Alright, well you know where to find me if you change your mind." Angela saunters off, trying to look carefree while I can here a few people who overheard what just happened giggling at her. I turn to face Anthony again, a big grin on my face.

"I'm sorry you had to deal with Angela, but man was that funny to watch." He smiles at me, chuckling softly.

"I'm guessing she does stuff like that a lot." I nod.

"Yeah, Angela is just one of those mean girls that people have to deal with. She thinks that she's a little princess who deserves everything she wants. Apparently, she wants you too. She's probably pouting right now since she can't have you." Anthony looks over to where Angela is sitting. As soon as he looks over, Angela turns her head away. She had obviously been watching us, and this just makes us laugh even harder. The joy is interrupted though when I hear a familiar voice coming from behind me.

"Hi Colomba." The smile immediately fades from my face, and I can see concern in Anthony's eyes when he sees this reaction. Turning around, I am greeted by the unpleasant sight of Alex. Oh gosh, I thought I was done with this guy for good. At junior prom last year, he had tried to make me kiss him and Luis told him off. He hasn't spoken to me since, and I thought he had learned his lesson that I don't want him around me. Apparently, I was wrong. I glare at Alex, making him look away from me with discomfort, but that doesn't stop him from talking to me.

"It's been a while since we've talked. I was hoping that I could see you over the summer, but I wasn't so lucky." Alex chuckles awkwardly, and I notice something a little odd about him. Before he had always been well kept up and always looking handsome, right now though he looks a bit disheveled and miserable. I'm not surprised though. From what I've been told, all his friends ditched him last year after everyone heard about what he tried to do with me. Even though he had always been a jerk, that was apparently their last straw and they ditched him. Alex must have had a really lonely summer, and from how people are currently glaring at him, I'm going to guess his senior year will be super lonely too. Even though I feel pity for him for being so lonely, I don't let myself feel bad for him. He does not deserve my sympathy after everything he has done.

"What do you want Alex?" I notice Alex flinch a little at my cold response, and from the corner of my eye I can see that Anthony is a little surprised by it too. When he looks at Alex though, I think Anthony is starting to understand why I am acting this way.

"Well, I was hoping we could talk and-" I turn away from Alex to face my friends again.

"We have nothing to talk about Alex. You tried to force me to kiss you last year, I don't want to speak with you again." Anthony's eyes grow wide with shock and fury when he hears that. The look he gives Alex after that is one of pure hatred.

"Please Colomba, just listen to me, I-"

"I believe that she just told you that she does not want to speak with you." Anthony interrupts, his voice calm, but his eyes signaling that Alex is in danger. My attention turns to Anthony, frightened that something might happen. I've heard about Alex beating people up before, and Alex is a pretty muscular guy. Anthony looks like he can handle himself against most people, but Alex might be a bit too much for him. At some of the surrounding tables, people have noticed the tense situation, and they have stopped eating to watch this. Alex glares down at Anthony who is still sitting calmly at the table.

"And who are you?" Alex growls with frustration at being interrupted. Anthony stands up, holding his hand out for Alex to shake like an old-fashioned gentleman.

"Anthony Amarelli. I would say it's a pleasure to meet you but that would be a lie, and I'm not a liar." Nat and I can't help but giggle hearing that, which only makes Alex's angered face become even more furious. His face is growing red with embarrassment when he notices that a few other tables around us are watching him be humiliated.

"Well, I wasn't talking to you, now was I?" Alex grumbles this as Anthony lowers his hand, knowing that Alex won't be polite and shake it.

"No, but it is obvious to anyone with an even slightly working brain that she isn't interested in speaking to you. She even told you plainly that she never wants to speak to you. Respect her wishes or else." My heart races as I notice Alex's hands clenching into tight fists.

"Alex, don't." I say this in a scolding tone, but Alex isn't even looking at me, he is standing toe to toe with Anthony, looking ready and willing to start a fight while Anthony is still standing there calmly.

"Or else what?" Alex growls at Anthony. Anthony does not answer Alex, Anthony is just looking at him like he is being a stupid kid. This only makes Alex even more enraged, and before anybody can do anything to stop him, Alex swings a punch at Anthony. My heart stops, thinking that Anthony will get hurt and this will turn into a mess of swinging fists all through the lunchroom. Everyone is surprised when that doesn't happen. When Alex's fist is only an inch from hitting Anthony in the face, his fist is stopped by Anthony catching it with one hand.

The entire cafeteria goes silent as Anthony remains calm, still holding on to Alex's fist while Alex is staring at him with complete shock. Alex opens his mouth like he is going to say something to

Anthony, but Anthony only needs to smirk at Alex to shut him up again. We all wait to see what happens, and we aren't disappointed. Anthony leans in a bit closer to Alex, and with the smirk still on his face, almost whispers something to him that I can thankfully still hear.

"I think you should probably leave now." I am so grateful that Alex is at least smart enough to take this advice. Anthony releases Alex's fist and Alex immediately turns around and walks away. As Alex starts the walk of shame to leave the cafeteria, most of the cafeteria breaks out into laughter. They laugh at Alex; they laugh at how stupid he was with all this. A few people also cheer for Anthony, happy that he put Alex in his place. When he sits down, Anthony gives me a pleasant smile full of warmth and comfort.

"Sorry about all that. I'm sure that he won't bother you anymore." I laugh a little, completely shocked by what has just happened.

"Oh my gosh, I can't believe you did that. I've never seen anybody stand up to Alex like that, everyone is too afraid of him." Anthony only chuckles at this remark.

"Well, of course I would. I could not let him make you uncomfortable. I won't let myself be afraid if someone is trying to hurt you." It feels as if all the pain I have ever felt in my life has disappeared the second he said that. I have never felt so close to a person I have just met, but with Anthony it feels like I have known him for years. Without even thinking about it, I hold him close in a tight embrace, and I never want to let him go.

"Thank you, thank you so much." I feel his strong arms wrap around me as I hear him whisper in my ear.

"You're welcome. I'll always be here to help you Colomba. I won't let anyone hurt you."

Chapter Four

Luis-
My Heart Is
Breaking

I'm getting to the lunchroom a little later than usual since I was talking to my art teacher, Mr. Sizemore. He has always been my favorite teacher, so it was nice to be able to catch up with him after everything that happened this summer. I packed my lunch today, so I thankfully don't need to stand in line. Alex rushes past me as I enter the cafeteria. Some laughter and cheering dies down as soon as he leaves the room, and Alex doesn't even bother to try making fun of me or anything as he passes by me. I only caught a quick glimpse of his face as he passed; was he crying? Oh well, he's not worth my time.

As I make my way towards the lunch table Nat, Colomba, Kaley, and I usually sit at, I stop dead in my tracks when I see an extra person there. A guy is sitting close beside Colomba, much too close. I don't know who this person is, but Colomba seems to know them pretty well. She is being very friendly to him. Whenever someone usually sits too close to her, she moves away, but she is letting him stay close to her.

The two of them are talking together and they look like they are hanging on to every word the other is saying. She is looking in his eyes as if she can't get enough. He is looking at her as if he is seeing an angel. She is an angel, but I don't like seeing him looking at her like that. Who is this guy?

Walking over to the table, Nat notices me and waves at me, but Colomba is too absorbed in her conversation with this guy to notice me. I will admit, that hurts to see. It's only when I am sitting in front of her that she notices me.

"Oh hey Luis. This is Anthony, he just moved here." This guy, Anthony, holds out his hand to me like he wants me to shake it. How old is this guy, forty or something? Why is he acting like he lived a hundred years ago or something? Feeling a bit awkward about it, I shake his hand.

"Nice to meet you, Luis." Anthony states. When I look in his eyes though, it feels like he is lying when he says that, like he doesn't really want me to be around him. Seeing how he was looking at Colomba though, he may be unhappy with me being around Colomba.

"Nice to meet you too, Anthony." From how he looks at me, I think he can tell that I'm lying too. Thankfully, Colomba doesn't seem to notice. She turns to Anthony, a perfect, friendly smile on her face.

"Luis has been our friend since we started high school. If you like anything that has to do with art, then you and Luis would get along." Anthony smiles warmly at her.

"I do have an appreciation for art. Some of my happier memories are of when I looked through some famous art museums in Europe. The best are in Paris, I believe." Colomba's eyes light up when he says that.

"You've been to Paris? I've always wanted to go there. Is it as beautiful as people say?" Anthony nods at her.

"Yes, it is, and the food is some of the best I've ever had." The two of them talk endlessly about art, music, and practically any other subject that comes to mind, all while Nat and I watch them. Nat is amused by them, while I feel as if I am watching my heart getting torn apart. After a while, Nat seems to realize how I am feeling since I see her glance over at me with pity in her eyes.

Near the end of lunch, Anthony takes his and Colomba's trays to turn them in to the lunch ladies. As soon as he is out of hearing range, Nat turns to Colomba with a sassy grin on her face.

"I know that I only date girls, but I would date him. He is that cute." Colomba playfully rolls her eyes at Nat.

"C'mon Nat, don't objectify him." Nat only laughs at this.

"Birdy, please, I can tell that you think he's handsome too, and that you like him." Colomba looks down at her hands in her lap, a blush forming on her cheeks.

"Well, yeah, I do like him, but I am attracted to him because of how he acts. He acts as if he is from another time, like he lived a hundred years ago or something. I find that really attractive." It feels like she has just stomped on my heart by saying that in front of me. Colomba looks back up at me, concern in her eyes.

"What do you think about him Luis? Do you think you guys could be friends? I think he likes hanging out with us, so you would probably see a lot of him. Do you think you would be comfortable with that?" I look away from her beautiful aquamarine eyes, feeling very uncomfortable with her questions. I want to say that I don't want him around, but of course they would ask why after that. I wouldn't be able to give them any kind of reason that would make sense. I just met the guy, how could I explain that I don't like him? It's not like I can say that I don't want him around since Colomba seems to like him. That would just make me look like a jerk. Knowing that I am kinda trapped in a corner with this, I have to lie.

"Oh yeah, I think that would be just fine. He seems really cool." Colomba smiles warmly at me. Usually that joyful smile would make me melt all over the floor, now it just makes my heart turn to ice since I know she is happy because I am welcoming another guy into our group. A guy that she seems to really care about. I want to throw up thinking about that.

Anthony returns to our table after this and the two start talking again. I try not to pay attention too much since I know it will just depress me. From the corner of my eye though, I can see Nat looking at me with both concern and pity. I don't look at her though, I don't want to feel her pity towards me.

When lunch ends, Colomba and Anthony keep talking as they start walking to their next classes. I watch them leave for a moment, seeing how happy she is with him while feeling miserable myself. I only watch them for a moment before I feel someone staring at me too. Looking to my side, I see Nat staring at me with the same pitying expression she had before. She starts moving closer, obviously so she can try to talk to me about what happened, but I walk away from her to head to my next class. I don't want to talk about what just happened. I don't want her to know exactly how I feel. I just want this day to end and hope that by tomorrow Colomba is no longer interested in this new guy.

As I leave the cafeteria, I hear a voice from behind me that makes my bad day feel even worse. Looking behind me, I see Alex approaching me, a cold, cruel grin on his face.

"What's up, freak?" Alex says to me with confidence even though I know he no longer has any power in this school. Rolling my eyes, I walk away from him. I don't even feel hurt by his words, just annoyed that he is even talking to me. Honestly, it's kinda hilarious to hear him call me freak. Everyone knows that nobody will talk to him anymore after what he did to Colomba at the end of last year. Right now, he's more of a social outcast than I ever was, and yet he's calling me a freak. That's just crazy and stupid.

Even though I am obviously not interested in what he has to say to me since I'm walking away from him, this idiot just runs up behind me so that he can start walking next to me. He grins at me like he knows something terrible about me and is enjoying every second of it,

"So freak, it looks like you're getting replaced." I don't say anything back to him, but I can feel my heart pounding in fury as Alex just continues to grin at me. From how happy he looks, I can easily see what he is talking about. He's talking about how Colomba was so interested in talking to Anthony instead of me. Was this complete weirdo just watching us during lunch to see this? How weird can you get? Since I don't respond to him, Alex seems to decide that he will keep going until he gets a reaction, just like he always did when he would pick on me.

"Seems like Colomba is a lot more interested in this new guy than she is with you. I'm not surprised though. A guy like you can easily get replaced. Who would want to hang out with a pathetic guy like you?" That finally gets me to stop walking to face him. I look at him, seeing how Alex now looks not so well kept anymore, how he looks like he hasn't slept well in ages and that he doesn't seem to be taking care of himself. Now he looks just as pathetic on the outside as he has always been on the inside. I look at Alex without any fear or anger anymore, all I can feel is annoyance knowing that this pathetic thing made me so miserable for so long.

"Just shut up you loser, nobody cares about what you think anymore." Alex's eyes grow wide with shock, and I don't give him any time to think of a comeback. This guy isn't worth my time, he never was. I let him control me even though he was nothing. How could I ever have let myself be hurt by him for so long? Even though I know that I shouldn't listen to him, I can't help but think about what he said. Am I being replaced?

I will admit that things have been a little weird ever since Colomba and I found out who we really are. We have been trying to act normal about all of this, but I can tell that we both still feel pretty awkward about things. I mean, we were enemies for a few years without even knowing it, and now I have switched to her side, and we are learning how to work with each other. It's hard enough being in group projects for school, but working together with superpowers is much, much harder. We train together most days after school, but it still feels weird. It was even weirder when we worked together the first time to help some people out of a burning car after a car crash. People were so happy to see her but were absolutely terrified to see me. She had to stop a few people from running away from me because, due to their panic, they tried to run back towards the fire. They would rather run towards fire than me. I've got to admit, that hurt a little.

When I think about how she and that Anthony guy were looking at each other, I can't help but feel pain because of it. For a while now, I have known that those who share the pins are destined to be together, Shadow told me that ages ago, so I know that we will be together one day so I shouldn't be worried. When I think about how happy she was looking at him, I can't help but wonder if maybe Shadow was wrong about this. The thought of that is really terrifying for me, but I have to know. I have to suffer through the last few classes of the day, and finally make it home before I can finally get some answers.

As soon as Uncle Diego finishes his countless questions about how my first day of school went, I head into my room so that I can have some privacy. Placing my hand over my Crow Medal, Shadow appears on my bed. She ruffles her feathers a bit before looking up at me with a happy face. Well, at least I think it's happy. It's really hard to tell how someone feels when they are a bird.

"Hello Luis, how was your first day?" I smile at her, feeling comforted being around my friend. I will admit that our relationship has been a lot better since I have joined Silver Dove's side. She is always ready to help me now and doesn't scold me anymore like she used to. Shadow even tells me that she is proud of me and happy with how I have turned myself around. I've got to admit that it feels wonderful hearing her say that. I feel like I am being praised by the parents I never really got to know.

"It was okay, but I think you saw what happened, and you probably know what I want to talk about." Shadow nods at this, understanding me completely.

"Yes, yes, I do. You are worried about this young man named Anthony. And I will admit, he makes me a bit nervous too. He looks a lot like someone I used to know who caused a lot of problems. There is something about him that makes me very concerned, but I know that I shouldn't judge him yet until we get to know him better." My eyes narrow in confusion as I look at her. Shadow never really talks about her past, so having her mention a bad person from her past is very strange. I've also never really seen her so uncomfortable before. What on earth could this person have possibly done to make Shadow, a creature that has lived for centuries, be afraid.

"Who was this person who caused all that trouble?" Shadow turns her head away from me to look out the window.

"Oh, it's not important. It would be impossible for them to be the same person since I knew that man ages ago, long before you were even born. It would be impossible for it to be him. What matters now is how you feel about this young man you currently know." I nod at this, knowing that no matter how many times I ask, she won't explain who this person was. She always changes the subject when she is done talking about something, and I don't want to make her upset, so I will go along with this.

"Yeah, I'm just worried about how Colomba was acting with him." Shadow cocks her head to the side in confusion.

"And what makes you so worried? She was friendly with him. Colomba is friendly with everyone, especially when that person is going through something. He is new to the school, maybe she was just being kind because of that. Do you think that there is something more?" Thinking back on how Colomba was looking into Anthony's eyes, I can't help but think that there really might be something more. There can't be though, can there? I shake my head, trying to get those dark thoughts out of my mind so that I can keep talking to Shadow.

"I don't get it Shadow; she was talking with him like she has a thing for him. She can't though, right? Colomba can't be in love with him, can she? She was just trying to be nice because he's new to the school, like you said, right?" Shadow only looks at me for a moment before she shrugs her wings at me.

"I cannot read her mind, Luis. I cannot give you the answers you want." I groan, feeling more frustrated than I ever have in my entire life. I have been frustrated before, but none of those things feel more important to me than Colomba.

"But she can't love him, right? I mean you told me that those who share the medals are destined to fall in love. Colomba and I are meant to fall in love. That's still true, right?" Shadow nods calmly at me.

"Yes, those who share the medals are destined to be together. That's all I can really say about this. I'm sorry that I don't have any more answers for you, Luis." My heart drops as a thought comes into my mind, something I hadn't really thought of before.

"Hey Shadow?" She tilts her head to the side in confusion, unsure of why she suddenly hears a bit of misery in my voice.

"Yes, Luis?" I sigh softly, afraid of the answer to my next question.

"You said that we will be together since we share the medals, but what if she actually doesn't love me? Is she going to be with me just because the medals force us to? Are the medals controlling how we feel? I mean, I fell in love with her before I got my medal, so I know how I feel is real, but does she feel the same? Maybe she is in love with this new guy. I don't want her to be forced to be with me just because the medals say we should. I couldn't do that to her. I don't want to force her to love me." Even though Shadow can't smile with a beak, I have a feeling that she is smiling at me.

"Do not worry Luis, the medals do not control your emotions. Just like with how the medals only work for those with a good heart, it can detect that good heart so that it will give you the powers. It will also find those whose hearts are meant to become one. It does not force anything. It only shows what is hidden within their hearts. You do not have to worry about anyone being forced to have feelings for another. The medals only show you what you may not realize at that time." It feels as if a huge weight has been lifted off my heart hearing her say that.

I look out my window, feeling joy as I watch the setting sun. At least I know that things are still fine, we will still be together one day. I do have to admit though, that I still feel mad thinking about her hanging out with Anthony like that. I know I sound jealous, and I am. I'm man enough to admit that I am jealous about this, but I can move past this. I will not control Colomba, I want her to be happy. If that means that she wants friends who are guys that I might feel a bit jealous about, then that's fine. That is something I need to work through. I won't try to hurt her just because of how I feel.

At least, that's what I am telling myself. As I keep thinking about them talking with each other, a dark gloominess settles over me. I can't help but thinking about them getting closer to each other, and my heart seems to grow colder at the thought of it. Misery seems to fill my soul as I think of them hanging out and possibly dating. What would I do if something like that happened? How could I still hang out with her and be friends if I have to see them acting like that with each other? I don't know if my heart could take that.

She is the most important person to me though, I'm sure I could stand it. I'm sure I could live with her caring for someone else if I can just be her friend. I'm sure I can live with that, right?

Chapter Five

Colomba-
My Heart Is
Happy

Making my way down the long driveway to my house after school, I enter through the front door with a huge smile on my face.

"Nonna, are you home?!" I call out, and I get an immediate response from the kitchen.

"Yes, how was your first day of school?" I head straight for the kitchen, eager to tell my grandmother about everything that happened today. Placing my bag on the kitchen table, I sit up on the counter as Nonna continues to make her homemade pasta.

"Today was wonderful. I love all my classes, and I met someone today." Nonna seems surprised by this announcement.

"You met someone new, that's strange for such a small school, I thought you would know pretty much everyone. Did they just move here?" I nod, eager to tell her everything about Anthony.

"Yes, he did, over the summer. His name is Anthony, and he is the most interesting guy I have ever met. He's so charming, and fun, and so very handsome. He kind of acts like those really cool guys in those old movies you show me. He's so charming, and he seems really interested in me too. We were talking with each other all through lunch, and he didn't really seem interested in any other girl." Nonna stops what she is doing so that she can look over at me. There is something in her gaze that I don't really understand, is that… concern?

"Really? This young man seems to have impressed you a lot in just one day." There's something in her voice that tells me that she doesn't really approve of Anthony, for some reason. Why is she judging him without knowing him? Nonna doesn't usually act like this. I pretend not to notice as I respond to her.

"Yeah, I mean he was able to tell off Angela and stood up to Alex and kept him from messing with me again. Alex tried to fight him, but Anthony stopped it with just one move. It was crazy impressive." Nonna nods at this. She did seem happy when I mentioned Anothny stopping Alex from messing with me, but there is still something dark in her eyes that I don't really understand.

"It sounds like you really care for this young man." A bit of sadness is in her voice when she says this, and I can't help but blush at her question. I look down, a bit embarrassed to look in her face as I answer.

"Yeah, I do. He's such a great guy Nonna. I know you will like him and approve of me dating him if that happens. He is a real gentleman, so I know that we could be happy together." I look back up to see that same look of concern on her face. It takes her a moment to finally ask the question that is obviously bugging her

"Well, what about Luis?" I look at her with confusion, not understanding what she means by that question.

"What about Luis?" She sets down the pasta she is making and takes a moment to wash her hands before she answers my question.

"What I mean is that those who share the medals are destined to be together. You have also told me before that the Crow had revealed that he has feelings for you. You now know that the Crow is actually Luis. Don't you think that it may hurt him to see you falling for someone else? Do you feel anything like that for him?" I look away from her, unsure of how to answer those questions. Looking out the back window, I can see our back garden. I stare at the tree for a moment where Luis had drawn my portrait only about two years ago. Has it really been that long?

I don't know how to answer those questions since I don't really know how I feel right now. Luis and I haven't really talked that much about what things were like for us before we found out who each other is. We have also never really talked about how people tell us we are supposed to end up together. It would be too weird to talk about. I have thought about how Luis would be a good boyfriend for someone, but I always thought he saw me as a friend, so I never let myself think of being that someone for him. How could I be with him after everything he has done? With Luis, everything is so confusing.

When I think about Anthony though, everything seems so clear. Anthony is so kind, gentle, and fun. I don't think he could ever do anything like what Luis did with his powers. If Anthony had these powers, he would probably only use them for good, and not for revenge. He could be someone I could truly care for.

Looking at Nonna though, I don't know if I can tell her all of that. She had been Silver Dove before me, and my grandpa had been the Crow. The medals had brought them together, and it's clear to see that Nonna had hoped that the medals would bring me to the one I love as well. I don't want to disappoint her, but I know that I have to tell her the truth.

"I don't know if that prophecy is true for Luis and I. After all the things he put me through with his powers, I don't know if I could be with him. Besides, Anthony is everything I have ever wanted from a guy. I'm not going to stop talking with him just because some people say Luis and I are supposed to be together just because we have these powers. That may have happened with you and Grandpa, but it may not be work for Luis and I." Nonna looks away, a bit sad about what I have just said. It hurts me a little knowing that I made her feel this way, but I need to be honest with her about how I feel. A bit of pity is in her eyes as she asks me something that makes me feel as if a rock was just thrown into my stomach.

"But Luis truly loves you, doesn't he?" I don't have an answer for her, so she keeps going. "I saw it since the first moment I saw you two together. Luis adores you. What will happen to him if you start dating someone else?" I take in a deep breath, knowing that what I am about to say will sound very cruel, but it will be the completely honest truth.

"Well if he really cared about me, he should have said something. He should have told me how he felt without having to wear a mask. He should have said it to my face and be honest with me. Instead, he went around my back, using his powers for bad things, and even now that we know who each other is, he still won't tell me how he feels even though he has told me before when he was just the Crow." I shake my head at the thought of all this. "If he wanted to be with me, then he should be honest and tell me. I won't wait around for him to grow a spine. I've found someone I like, I won't turn him down for a guy who can't even be honest with me." When I see the pain in Nonna's eyes, I feel bad about having to say all that, but I can't keep anything from her. Hopping off the counter, I grab my bag and start heading to my room.

"I'm going to start reading a book we will be working on in English class. I'll talk to you later, Nonna." I leave without another word. I had been so happy when I came in the house to tell her about Anthony. Now I just feel depressed as I keep having thoughts about Luis. I don't know what to do to make Nonna feel better, but I won't let myself hide how I really feel just to make other people happy. I did that for the longest time, and it only caused me problems. I won't let myself do that anymore. I want to be happy, and I won't let some stupid prophecy get in the way of that. I start reading the book for English class, but I don't really absorb anything that's being said, I am too busy thinking about what Nonna said and the two guys that are now a big part of my life.

Chapter Six

Luis-
Gym Class

Standing in the gym in the shorts and T shirt we are required to wear, I feel awkward and uncomfortable being here. I'm an artsy guy, not a gym guy. It feels so unfair that the school makes us take gym class at least once while we are in high school. I waited until senior year because I was hoping the rule would change and I could get out of it. I was wrong. Now I am stuck in this gym, just hoping and praying that I won't have to do much to pass this class. I would rather be working on my art projects or finishing homework than doing the stupid games and such they will make us do here.

One other thing that is really annoying about this is that I share this class with someone I don't really like. I only really noticed today that I have this class with that guy Anthony that I met yesterday. I guess I didn't really notice him before since I didn't know who he was the other day, but now I am just annoyed. The gym teacher is currently just telling us the different kinds of activities we can do today, and Anthony is about ten feet away from me listening to them with all his attention and respect. A few feet away from him, I can see a group of girls looking at him and whispering to each other as they giggle. I can tell that they are talking about Anthony, and it's clear from how they are giggling that they think he's very attractive. Actually, I can see quite a few people sneaking peeks at him as if they are looking at a celebrity. I guess since Drew's Hollow is such a tiny town that when a new person arrives they kind of are a celebrity, everyone wants to know them. I try to keep my eyes away from him though, I don't want to even think about that guy. Every time I look at him, all I can think about is how Colomba was talking to him yesterday. It makes my stomach churn just thinking about it.

As the gym teacher finishes whatever it is they were saying, everyone starts breaking off into groups to try and figure out what they want to do with their friends, leaving me by myself. Staring down at my feet, I get the feeling that this class will be a very lonely one for me this year. When I think that, I notice another pair of feet stopping right next to me, I look up to see Anthony standing next to me, a warm smile on his face.

"Hey, you're Luis, right? I'm Anthony, we met yesterday at lunch, remember?" I try to smile back at him, but with how I feel about him, it probably looks more like a grimace than anything else.

"Yeah, I remember you. What's up Anthony?" He points over to a group of people who are looking over at us expectantly.

"Me and a few others are going to play volleyball if you would like to join us?" I blink a few times, not sure if I actually heard him right. Did he just try to include me in a game with other people? The only other person who has done something like this for me is Colomba and Nat. I nod my head at him, still not sure if this is actually happening to me.

"Sure." Anthony's smile grows wider at hearing me say that.

"Great, c'mon let's go." I follow him to join the group of people we will be playing with as we all go to claim one of the volleyball nets and a ball. We all introduce ourselves, and I can't help but look at Anthony with a bit of confusion. Just yesterday I had absolutely hated this guy, now when I look at him though, I'm starting to feel a bit differently. I mean, this guy is actually trying to be nice to me and include me in this game. That never really happens to me at all, it almost feels like I am in a dream. Maybe I was wrong about this guy. Maybe he is actually a good guy. I can only wonder how things will go between him and Colomba, but maybe the two of us could actually be friends. I only really have friends who are girls, maybe it will be nice to have a friend that's a guy.

Our little group organizes where everyone will position themselves for the game. Anthony and I are on a team, and he positions himself behind me on the opposite side of the volleyball court, while I am up front near the net. Anthony is given the ball to do the first serve, and I face forward so that I can observe the other team, ready for the game to start. From behind me, I hear Anthony hitting the ball to start the game, for a moment, I wonder why I don't see the ball going over the net, and then I realize why. A sharp pain hits the back of me head and a loud smacking sound seems to echo throughout the gym as I let out a little yelp of shock and pain. Looking behind me, I see the volleyball bouncing away from me as Anthony looks at me with an expression of guilt and surprise. He holds his hands up to eye level like he is showing me that he is surrendering. That does not stop me from feeling the rage growing inside of me. It feels like lava is flowing through my veins right now.

That guy just hit me with the ball! He did that on purpose, didn't he?! My face is growing warm, and I can tell that my face must be crazy red in my rage. From the corners of my eyes, I can see some of the other people in the gym looking at the two of us, wondering (and also a little afraid) to see what will happen between the two of us. I don't care about them though. I only care about the jerk who just hurt me.

"What was that for Anthony?!" I yell at him, making everyone in the gym now turn their attention towards us. Anthony lowers his head in shame in response, looking truly guilty, but something in the back of my mind says that he isn't being honest.

"I'm really sorry Luis, I didn't mean to do that. I've just never played this game before. I didn't mean to hurt you, it was an accident." His voice sounds quiet and pitiful, almost like he is afraid of my anger, not something I would ever expect from a guy like him. What is going on here? A few people begin gathering around Anthony, looking at me with disgust and anger.

"Yeah, what's your problem Luis, it was obviously an accident. Why are you being such a jerk to Anthony?" I stay silent, not really sure what I can say. They all turned on me so quickly. All around me, I can see people glaring at me like I am being the bad guy here. Am I wrong? Was that an accident? It honestly seemed like he meant it. I know that I can't say that though since everyone will get mad at me. Instead, I stare down at my feet as I finally find the courage to speak again.

"Sorry Anthony. I didn't mean to get mad at you, that just really hurt." Anthony accepts my apology with a smile while everyone else goes back to what they were doing before. I can tell that Anthony may have forgiven me, but nobody else has. They are still looking at me like I'm the villain.

As we continue on with our game, I can hear a few people saying bad things about me to their friends. I used to try and ignore these kinds of things, but ever since things have gotten better for me (I have friends now, Alex doesn't mess with me, and since Alex isn't doing his usual stuff nobody else seems interested in messing with me) I find it hard to ignore these things. Everything has been going well for so long now, nobody makes fun of me anymore, so it really hurts to hear them bad mouth me again.

As the game goes on, I keep my mouth shut as a few questions race through my mind. Was that really an accident, or did he want to cause me some pain? If he did, then why did he want to do that? Is it because he could tell that I like Colomba too? Does he want to show me that everyone likes him more so

I should back off?

I don't know what's going on here, but I think my safest bet is to just let things play out. I need to see if he will try anything else against me. If he does, then I know that something is really wrong here. I just need to be patient, and hope that everything will be alright again soon.

Chapter Seven

Colomba-
An Amazing
Surprise

Sitting in a field on my family's property, I wait for Luis to show up. Ever since we found out who we really are, we meet at this field to practice using our powers together. I am my regular self right now, enjoying the feeling of the wind on my face. I want to feel relaxed before I have to transform into Silver Dove and get all sweaty and gross. Right now, everything just feels so right. It has been about two weeks since school started, and everything feels so perfect.

I've been hanging out a lot with Anthony lately. Whenever we both have free time, we try our best to spend that time together. No matter how much time we spend together we never seem to get bored with each other. I can't believe I've met someone like him. He just seems so perfect to me.

I am worried about one thing though, Luis. Ever since we met Anthony on that first day of school, he's been acting different. It's almost like he hates Anthony or something, but he won't say it out loud. Whenever Anthony sits with us at lunch, Luis doesn't really talk much, almost like he doesn't want to be part of the conversation if Anthony is there. I don't know what's up with him. Is he upset that Anthony has joined our little group? I mean, for the longest time it was just me, him, and Nat. Does it feel uncomfortable for him to have one more person joining us? Is he really so jealous about us having more friends? I bet they could be good friends if Luis just gave him a chance, but Luis doesn't even seem to want to try. Oh well, he will have to get used to it some day since I don't plan on kicking Anthony out of my life just to make someone else more comfortable. I won't let someone else's feelings control my life. For now, we just need to focus on being Silver Dove and the Crow so that we can keep the world safe. As long as we can do that together then I'm sure we can be fine.

It doesn't take long before I see a dark figure flying through the air. I wave up at it, and seconds later, Luis as the Crow lands only twenty feet in front of me. The smile fades from my face when I see a bit of anger on Luis' face. What's going on? Did he have a bad day today or something?

"Hey Luis, what's up?" He only glances up at me for a moment before his gaze returns to his feet.

"Nothing." There is some irritation in his voice that makes me feel a bit hurt, knowing that he is letting some of his anger out on me.

"Um, Luis I can obviously tell that something is up. You seem pretty angry, is something wrong?" He looks into my eyes and sighs, releasing the anger from his face.

"You've been hanging out a lot with that new guy, Anthony, I just feel like… you know-" Actually, I don't know, but maybe he feels like I am not giving him enough attention or that I am ignoring him. I guess I was right about Luis having bad feelings about Anthony. Something in the back of my mind tells me that he feels like he is being replaced by Anthony, but he couldn't feel that way. How could he feel like that when we are the only ones who have the power of the pins and work together to fight evil? Plus he is one of my best friends, he could never be replaced.

"I'm sorry if you feel like I was ignoring you, I just want to make him feel welcomed since he is new to town. You should talk with him more at lunch, he's a really cool guy, and if you got to know him you both could be really good friends." He looks down at his feet again, disbelief all over his face, as if he thinks that he could never be friends with Anthony. What is really going on with Luis? He is acting so weird lately.

"Yeah, I don't know Colomba, I-" Luis suddenly stops talking as a shadow falls over both of us and quickly disappears, like something large just flew over us. We both look up, our conversation forgotten, and I can see something huge flying right towards us. Luis steps in between me and whatever that is, spreading his wings out to try and defend me from this mysterious thing. Even though his mask is on, I can still see that he is absolutely terrified. As this thing gets closer to us, a strange thought pops into my head. I don't feel afraid right now, ever since I got the Dove Pin, whenever danger is about to happen, I know it, the pin warns me about it. Right now though, I don't feel that, I feel fine. Something in my mind tells me that this thing will not harm us. I don't say it out loud though, I could be wrong. It is better to be safe than sorry when it comes to situations you don't understand.

When it is only a few yards from landing, the sunlight hits it just right, and I am almost blinded by a golden light coming off of it. I shield my eyes with my hand. When I hear the thing land, the golden light seems to die down and Luis and I look at something that makes my heart stop for a moment.

Someone wearing golden armor like a medieval knight stands only ten feet from us, a helmet covering their face, but that isn't what makes my jaw drop when I look at them. Sticking out of their back is a set of large, golden wings. Luis and I look at each other for a moment before returning our gaze back to him. I can tell that we are both thinking the same thing; there is someone else like us? They must have a medal or something like us to be able to have those wings. What is going on here?

As Luis and I stare in shock at this person, they begin to walk towards us. I can hear Luis gasp softly in fear as he immediately springs into action and rushes towards the guy. He raises his fist just as the guy reaches out his hand, obviously for a handshake. Luis freezes when he sees this, looking at the guy behind the knight's helmet, then down at the hand that is held out in front of him. I can hear the guy behind the helmet laugh softly when he sees Luis' confusion.

"You afraid of a friendly greeting Luis?" Luis jumps back a little in surprise at hearing this strange person referring to him by name, but what really surprises me is that I recognize the voice. Slowly and cautiously stepping forward, I speak to them, my voice coming out softly, almost as if I am nervous about what I may find out.

"Anthony? Is that you?" Luis looks back at me, and then back at the person in the suit of armor with what almost looks like horror. Why is he looking at them like that? The figure uses both of their hands to lift off the helmet to reveal that it really is Anthony beneath the armor. He smiles teasingly at Luis.

"What is it, Luis? It looks like you've seen a ghost." Anthony laughs again, making Luis' cheeks grow red with anger. I step forward towards them, Luis looks a little afraid when he sees me do this, almost as if he is afraid that Anthony will do something bad to me. How could he think like that? Anthony is our friend, yet he's acting like he is our enemy. This may have been a surprise for us, but we shouldn't act like he is a danger to us just because we are confused. Despite Luis acting this, Anthony is smiling at the both of us warmly.

"Is it really you Anthony? How on earth did you get powers like us? And how did you know it is us behind these masks?" Anthony walks up to me, standing right in front of me, making Luis look even more concerned and frightened than before. Seriously, what is up with Luis today?

"I'm guessing I got my powers the same way you guys did. Someone gave me a medal that gives me powers." He chuckles as he gives me a charming smile. "It honestly wasn't too hard to figure out you were Silver Dove, I mean you have the same determination, good heart, and power that Silver Dove showed in all the videos people have showed me. Plus, your name Colomba, which literally translates to dove in Italian, so it wasn't that hard." Behind us, I can see Luis blushing a bit in embarrassment. He probably feels that way since Anthony has only known me for only two weeks and was able to figure it out, while it took Luis almost three years.

"Well what kind of powers do you have as… whoever you are?" Luis asks with a bit of venom in his voice. I swear, why is Luis being so rude right now? Anthony seems to pretend not to notice the angry tone in Luis' voice though, which I am grateful for. I mean, we just found out that there is someone else with superpowers, I want them to be a friend and ally to us, not become our enemy just because someone is being rude today. I'm glad that out of the two of them, one can be mature and kind, unlike Luis.

"I am Golden Eagle. When I transform, I get a bow." He reaches behind himself and pulls out a golden bow, but without any arrows. He pulls at the string like he is getting ready to fire it, and a golden arrow magically appears there. When he relaxes the string, the arrow disappears, and he puts the golden bow back in the holder on his back. "And I can also create anything that I can think of."

He waves his hand gently through the air and a little golden dove and a golden crow start flying through the air. The little dove gently flutters its wings and flies over to me, cooing softly and nuzzling its head against my cheek in a loving way. The crow is not as friendly though. It swoops at Luis, making Luis cover his face with his arms in fear. The golden crow disappears before it can hurt him though, making Luis' face grow red with embarrassment again. Anthony playfully smirks at this, probably getting his bit of revenge on Luis for being mean earlier. My little dove disappears as well, and I'm a bit sad to see it go, while Luis is pretty livid.

"What was that for?!" Luis screams at him, rage making his usually soft voice sound almost cruel. Almost like the voice he had used as the Crow when he was still fighting against me. It actually sends a shiver of discomfort and even a bit of fear down my spine to hear it.

"C'mon Luis, he was just teasing you. It didn't even touch you, it just spooked you a little. You kind of deserve it for being so rude a second ago." Luis looks down at me, he almost appears hurt that I am not siding with him. It looks like he is about to say something, but decides not to, choosing to remain silent instead. I turn back around to face Anthony, a welcoming smile on my face.

"That is a really cool power. I bet you can do some pretty crazy stuff with that. I'm sure everyone in town will be happy to have you join our side." I'm about to shake Anthony's hand to welcome him into our tiny group of heroes, when I feel Luis grab my other hand. He isn't looking at me though, he faces Anthony, his face full of held back anger.

"Excuse us a minute." Without warning, he pulls me by the hand over to the side, far enough away that Anthony won't hear us when Luis speaks to me.

"What are you doing? Letting him into the group without knowing a thing about him? He could be a complete psycho for all we know. We need to be more careful about this. He could turn on us as soon as our backs are turned. We should at least give him a test or something." Oh my gosh, I am getting tired of Luis having this thing against Anthony. Luis seems to hate him for no reason since Anthony hasn't done a thing to him except be nice.

"Knock it off Luis, this isn't funny. We may have only known him for a little bit, but he has only shown us that he is a good person. We should give him a chance. Besides, the medals only work for those with a good heart, remember?" I can tell that Luis wants to keep arguing about this but isn't sure about what he can say back to that. He knows that I am speaking the truth. "And let's not forget that I let you join my side and forgave you after everything you have done, so we should let him have a chance too." Luis seems angry and embarrassed that I brought up his past acting as the villain in our school, but he knows he can't argue with me about it since he knows I'm right. I turn back to walk over to Anthony.

"Welcome to the group Anthony." We shake hands, but Anthony gives Luis a concerned look.

"Thank you, but are you sure you are both alright about this? I don't want to make anyone uncomfortable." I glance back at Luis who looks away at me, obviously feeling uncomfortable since he was judging Anthony so hard a second ago, and now Anthony is being super polite to him.

"Don't worry, he's just worried about letting someone in on our secrets too quickly, but you already gave us your biggest secret by taking off your mask, so I'm sure we can trust you." Anthony smiles at me warmly, and it feels like I'm going to melt all over the grass.

I can't believe how lucky I am. The guy I really like is now part of our little group. Everything is so perfect right now. I smile, trying to hide how embarrassed I feel as I ask Anthony something.

"Well, how about you show us some of the things you can do?" His smile grows even larger, showing off his perfect white teeth, eager to show off his powers to us.

"I would be delighted to."

Chapter Eight

Luis-
A New
Threat

I can't believe this is happening.

I can't believe that this guy has powers like us.

We just ended practice a little bit ago, and I just got back home. I am pacing up and down my room as Shadow watches me, perched on top of my bed. Even she looks nervous right now. I can tell by how her feathers are all ruffled.

"Can you believe this Shadow? How does this guy have powers like us? I thought that there were only two medals like ours. What gives?" Shadow nods at me, understanding my confusion.

"At the beginning of these medals, there were three. Those with the medals worked together to try and bring peace to the world, but years ago, what would be ages for you, but only moments for me, someone with Anthony's medal tried to use his medal to unite the world under his rule." Shadow pauses for a moment, sadness coming over her as if she is reliving some horrible memory. "He had seen how evil the world could be, and he wanted to use his powers to make sure it would never happen again by being in charge of all of it. The other two with the medals defeated him and that medal was lost. I thought that I would never see it again. It explains why I felt so strangely towards Anthony. I had sensed the medal on him but couldn't believe he could have it. It is nice to see it again in different hands." Shadow looks off at nothing as if she is lost in thought while I look away from her to look out my window. So it is true; his medal is the same as ours. We aren't the only ones to share the medals now.

My heart skips a beat as horror comes over me. Things might be even worse than I had thought before.

"Shadow?" She seems to perk herself out of her deep thought when she hears me say her name.

"Yes Luis?" I take in a deep breath, knowing that this will be a difficult question for me to ask since I might get an answer that I don't like.

"You had told me that those who share the medals are destined to be together. Does that mean that she could now fall in love with Anthony instead of me since he has a medal too?" I feel my eyes grow warm as I hold back the tears, waiting for her to answer me. Shadow releases a faint sigh as she looks down at her talons, obviously not wanting to look at me when she gives me her answer.

"Yes, she could end up with Anthony instead of you." I turn away from her as I feel the tears beginning to fall down my face.

"Why did you tell me that she would love me if

you knew that she could end up with someone else?" I hear Shadow fly off of my bed and land on my shoulder, using her beak, she gently pushes the hair out of my face like she always does whenever she is trying to comfort me.

"I told you that because I thought it was true." I turn my head so that I can't see her, but she just starts flying right in front of my face so that she can look me in the eyes as she speaks to me. "When the Golden Eagle Medal went missing, that meant that nobody could wear it, meaning that they wouldn't fall in love with whoever is wearing the other medals. I thought that it was just you and Colomba with the medals, so I thought it would work out like this. I'm sorry that I turned out to be wrong." Looking into her black eyes I can't help but let my anger show to her.

"You're supposed to be the guardian of these medals, how could you not tell that he has one?" Shadow perches herself on my shoulder again, her head hanging in shame at her failure.

"Honestly, that mistake has been bothering me as well recently." She sighs, remaining silent for a moment before continuing her statement. "I guess I didn't realize it because I wasn't expecting it. I could sense that there was something different about him, but I thought the medal was gone so I just didn't guess that. I suppose we will just have to live with all this and let it happen." I take in a deep breath to prevent myself from crying more.

"But how can I live with this if it means that I might lose Colomba to him?" Shadow looks in my eyes with absolute seriousness as she replies to me.

"You can't lose her if you never really tried to

have her." Without another word, Shadow flies off my shoulder soars right into the medal on my chest, disappearing. She leaves me alone with a broken heart and so many unanswered questions. That is how I spent the rest of the evening.

Now I am back at school and Colomba, Nat, Anthony, and I are finishing up lunch and heading to our next classes. Colomba and Anthony are happily chatting while Nat and I hang behind them. I watch those two with both a fire in my veins and an overwhelming amount of pain. I am so wrapped up in what I see that it takes me a moment to realize that Nat said something to me.

"I'm sorry, Nat, what did you say?" Nat rolls her eyes at me playfully.

"I was asking, what's wrong with you? You look like the world is ending or something." I can't help but chuckle at Nat. She's a lot closer to the answer than she thinks. When I look at Colomba and Anthony, my world crumbles around me.

"I don't want to say it, you'll just laugh at me." Nat narrows her eyes in confusion.

"What do you mean? Just tell me so I can at least try to help." I sigh, knowing that Nat is one of the only people I can talk to about this, she's known how I've felt about Colomba since the beginning, but I'm still afraid to say it out loud.

"I guess I'm just… upset about how Colomba is acting around Anthony." Nat looks at me with annoyance in her dark eyes before she brings up one of her hands to start rubbing her forehead like she's really frustrated with me.

"Upset? Really, Luis? I think the word you're

looking for is jealous." Even though I know what she is saying is true, I still get mad.

"I'm not jealous!" I look around awkwardly to make sure nobody is looking at us when I realize that I had yelled that. Thankfully nobody seems to care about what we are talking about. Nat just rolls her eyes at me in her annoyance.

"Oh, c'mon Luis, it's not like you've been hiding it well. You've been acting like a jerk to Anthony even though he has done nothing to you, and you are even avoiding Colomba whenever she is around him. Colomba is still clueless of course, but even Anthony seems to have figured it out, and I haven't even told him how you care for her. It's obvious Luis, you love her and you're losing her, so you're jealous. Just admit it." I look down at my shoes, knowing that she's right. Nat is one of the few people in this world that I can't hide from.

"Okay fine, but I don't know what to do about it." Nat surprises me with a very simple answer.

"There's nothing you can do Luis. You lost. That's it, move on." I look back up at her, pain striking my heart.

"What are you talking about? What do you mean I've lost?" Nat shrugs at me as if the answer to my question is obvious.

"I mean exactly what I said, Luis. You lost." I feel my heart begin to race as anger rushes through me.

"And what do you mean by that?" Nat just groans with frustration at my question.

"Do you really need me to spell it out for you?" Nat looks me dead in the eyes with complete seriousness in her voice.

"You lost. You could have told Colomba how you felt about her a million times. You've known and liked her ever since we started high school, and now you're getting mad in our senior year when she starts liking another guy? C'mon Luis, did you just expect for her to always be single, waiting for you to finally stop being a coward and actually tell her how you feel?" Nat shakes her head at me with a bit of pity coming into her eyes. "You kept yourself stuck in one spot and she moved past you, she found someone else. You've got to either tell her how you feel now before they officially start dating, or it will happen, and you will lose your chance. So, what will it be? Are you going to finally be brave about this, or are you going to regret this for the rest of your life?" I look down at my shoes unable to look at her.

"Do you really think the two of them will start dating?" Nat sighs, probably annoyed right now that she has to explain everything to me.

"Well yeah, the two of them obviously like each other. They hang out all the time, they can talk about anything together and not get bored, they have similar interests, and they have a lot of fun together. Only an idiot would think they don't like each other. So, make your move now Luis, or else you will lose what may be your last chance to finally be with her." I look back up at her, fear making my heart race.

"What do you mean it could be my last chance?" Nat looks at me like I'm being stupid.

"We are seniors Luis; this is our last year in high school. Some of us will go away for college after this, and you know Colomba will go to college since she wants to be a doctor. Once high school ends you may never see her again, she might move far away for college, you don't know. So, you can tell her how you feel now, and may get a chance to be with her, or you stay quiet like you have the past three years and will always be left wondering what would have happened if you actually tried for once." I bury my face in my hands as I feel myself starting to panic.

"But I don't know if I can do it, Nat." She pauses for a moment, the silence hanging between us is as heavy as a mountain. Through my fingers I can see her looking at me with pity in her eyes before she gives me a heartbreaking bit of advice.

"Then move on Luis." I feel my eyes beginning to burn as I hold back the tears that threaten to fall down my face.

"But I can't do that either Nat, she has been everything for me for so long. She is just so perfect that I don't think I'm worthy of her. How can I ask her out when I am nothing compared to her?" Nat groans beside me and starts walking ahead of me. I lower my hands from my face to see that she is still walking away from me but has her head turned back over her shoulder to look at me, her face is twisted into a mask of disappointment and frustration.

"You know what Luis, just forget it. I have been trying to convince you to do this for years, and you have done nothing. If you want to be with her then take a chance and ask her out. Will you fail? Maybe. Your other option though is to keep doing nothing and regret your decision, possibly for the rest of your life. Now just ask yourself which you would rather live with because I am tired of being the shoulder you cry on and yet you do nothing to fix your own problems." Without another word, Nat walks down the hallway, turning down another hall, leaving me alone in the crowd of people heading to their next class. She leaves me alone with my thoughts. That's probably one of the cruelest things you can do to me, leaving me by myself, leaving me with my worst enemy.

I keep walking to my next class, my head hanging and my feet dragging underneath me. I make it to my class without any issues, but I just rest my head on my desk, not even looking around me. I can hear the teacher starting class and they talk about something having to do with science, but I don't pay attention. I am too lost in my own thoughts, too lost in my misery.

Chapter Nine

Colomba-
Telling
Nonna

I leave the bus with two extra people today. Anthony said that he would come home after school today with me to meet Nonna. When I had told him that my grandmother had the Dove Pin before me and was Silver Dove when she was younger, he was very excited to meet her.

I had invited Luis to come with us as well, he said he would be happy to do it. Honestly, he didn't really look happy to come along though. He almost looks like a kid being forced to tag along to do something they hate. I swear, Luis is acting like such a whiney little baby recently. I'm getting really tired of it. He just needs to get over whatever it is that's bothering him since I think it's starting to get on everyone's nerves. After lunch, even Nat seemed annoyed with him, and Nat is probably one of the most patient people I know. The two even refused to speak to each other on the bus, so you know it's serious if they're doing that. Neither of them explained what is going on between them though, so I didn't ask about it. I could tell that they wouldn't tell me even if I did ask anyway. I don't want to get involved in things that aren't my business. I don't want to be nosey… Okay maybe I do want to be nosey, but I won't, I don't want to hurt my friends' feelings or make them uncomfortable. I would feel terrible doing that to them.

The three of us; Anthony, Luis, and I, walk up the driveway to my little stone home with its huge flower garden in the front and a little swing hanging from a tree out front. Anthony smiles when he sees it.

"You have a very beautiful home." I smile back at him, hearing the sincerity in his voice.

"Thank you, my grandfather built it himself when he and my grandmother came to this country." Anthony looks at the house with admiration, his eyes going over every detail.

"He did a very good job, I'm very impressed." It warms my heart to hear him compliment my grandfather's work. As I thank him, I can see Luis behind us looking annoyed and uncomfortable. I swear, I'm not going to let this guy's bad mood bother me today. I'm too happy about everything to let that happen.

The three of us come in through the front door and I shout out, "Nonna, are you home?! I have someone here that I want you to meet!" It only takes a moment for us to hear the answer.

"Yes Tesoro, I'm in the sewing room!" I lead the

way for us, heading to the sewing room. I'm the first to enter the room. Nonna is holding a quilt she is working on, a bright smile on her face when she sees me.

"Hello Tesoro, I hope you had a wonderful day. Now who is this person you are so excited to introduce me to?" I smile even brighter as I feel myself blush in joy.

"Nonna, this is Anthony, the guy I told you about, the one who now has the Golden Eagle Medal." Anthony enters the room, and the bright smile that had been on Nonna's face immediately disappears to be replaced by absolute terror. She is looking at Anthony as if she is seeing a demon. She opens her mouth as if she is about to speak, but nothing comes out. I can see her legs shaking and I rush over to put my arm around her to keep her steady as I lead her over to a chair. As I do this, she never takes her eyes off Anthony, as if she is scared that he will do something to her if she stops looking at him. I look over at Luis and Anthony. Luis looks concerned by what is going on but doesn't seem to know what to do. Anthony looks both concerned for my grandmother and also a bit hurt that my grandmother is so terrified of him.

When I finally get Nonna to sit in a chair, she takes her eyes off of Anthony to look at me with betrayal and horror.

"How could you do this? How could you bring Matteo Greco into this home?" I feel my eyes narrow in confusion. What on earth is she talking about?

"Nonna, who is Matteo Greco?" Anthony finally steps forward a bit, but is respectful and stays far from Nonna to make sure that she stays comfortable.

"You don't have to worry Ma'am. Matteo Greco was my grandfather, my name is Anthony Amarelli." This seems to calm Nonna down slightly, but she still seems concerned about Anthony, like he is a bomb that can go off at any second.

"Good, I had hoped that I would never see that man again. No offense to you or your grandfather." Anthony hangs his head in shame, obviously taking offense to what she said, while Luis and I remain confused.

"Nonna, who is Matteo Greco? And why are you so afraid of him?" Nonna lets out a faint sigh before she speaks, a deep sadness in her voice.

"Matteo Greco used to be a friend of your grandfather and I when we were young. During the war, while we were still in Italy, we all found out that we had these medals that gave us powers, so we decided that we would use these powers to help fight the Nazis." She takes a deep breath, trying to calm herself after her little shock earlier so she can tell us this story. "When the war was over, your grandfather and I were engaged, and we thought that Matteo would possibly join us so that we could continue our fight to keep peace in the world." Nonna pauses for a moment, shuddering a little as a deep pain came into her eyes from these dreadful memories.

"We were wrong. Matteo had seen all the pain that the war had caused and thought that the world needed a strong ruler who could make sure that nothing like that could ever happen again. He thought that he could be that ruler." Confusion seems to fill both Luis and I at this, but Luis is the first to speak up.

"But how could the medal still work for him if he's going after world domination like a cartoon super villain?" Nonna looks at Luis with disbelief in her eyes, as if she can't believe he's the one asking this.

"The medal could still see that he had a good heart, his intention was to make the world better. He just thought that the best way to do that was to have him rule it. I suppose it works just like how the medal kept working for you even after what you did the past few years." A very uncomfortable silence follows this, and none of us can look at each other as Nonna looks at Luis with a bit of anger. She likes Luis, don't get me wrong, but she still feels a bit upset with him for what he put me through our first few years of high school. Luis looks embarrassed, and almost as if he might cry at her words. Nobody comforts him though, he kind of deserved that to be honest. Nonna lets the silence hang between us for a moment before continuing.

"Your grandfather and I couldn't let this happen. We had already seen so many people die, we did not want another war to start over this. We battled against him, but he had the strongest medal out of the three of us. He could create anything that he imagined, and Matteo had a very powerful imagination. He created this portal into darkness and tried to get us into it, but we were able to get him in it instead. Matteo had said that there would be no way to get out if we got trapped in there, so I thought that he would die in that portal, and we would never see him or his medal again." We all look at Anthony, all of us silently signaling to him that it is now his turn to explain things. Anthony nods his head, a bit of discomfort in his eyes. It's clear that he knows that he has to talk about this, but he really doesn't want to.

"Yeah, I will admit my grandfather did do some very bad things. I will apologize for him since he isn't alive anymore." Nonna hangs her head, a bit of disappointment in her eyes. I can tell that she feels sad knowing that her old friend is gone, even though their last memory together was not a good one. "He got out of that portal thing after a few days and realized that he was wrong for what he tried to do. He decided to live a quiet life after that, He met my grandmother and had a small family. He never even used his medal again after that. He didn't even tell me about all of this until he was about to die. He gave it to me and said that he hoped that I would use it more wisely than him. He died right after saying that." Anthony hangs his head, misery clouding his gaze. Gently taking his hand in mine, I give it a gentle squeeze. He looks back up at me with a grateful smile. With this bit of encouragement, he is able to look at Nonna again.

"I hope that you can accept me, Ma'am. Colomba is very important to me, and I know how important you are to her. I don't want any bad feelings between us." My heart leaps when I hear him say that I am important to him. Nonna glances down at our hands, and only now do I realize that he is still holding mine. She smiles softly at the two of us, knowing that he is speaking the truth when he tells her that I am important to him.

"Alright, I cannot get mad at you for the sins of

your grandfather. I can only hope that you will use your powers more wisely than him."

Anthony and I smile at each other, knowing that we have my Nonna's approval. I can't even put into words how happy this makes me. If we have her approval for this, then I'm sure she would approve of us dating someday.

Something behind Anthony catches my eye though, bringing a bit of gloom over this joyful moment. Luis is looking at the two of us with an expression I have never seen before on him. It is a mixture of jealousy and anger. What's going on? It almost looks like he is mad that Anthony got Nonna's approval. Why is he acting like this? Why has he been like this lately?

Oh well, I won't let his sour mood affect me. I am happy now, and if that bothers Luis then he will have to deal with it. I am not responsible for his emotions.

The four of us begin to talk, Nonna mostly trying to get to know Anthony more, while Luis just mopes a little in the corner while the rest of us talk. Something in the back of my mind tells me that I should be concerned by how he feels considering how he has acted in the past with his powers when he got upset, but I shouldn't think that way. Luis has changed, he is using his powers for good now, he won't do anything like that again... At least, I hope not.

Chapter Ten

Luis-
More Sad
Words

As I hurry to try and get ready for school before the bus arrives, Shadow watches me as I quickly stuff things into my backpack.

"Luis, can I speak to you about something?" I don't stop what I am doing as I respond to her.

"Sure, just be quick I need to run out to get on the bus soon." She doesn't waste a second and says something that actually gets me to stop what I'm doing.

"You need to look out for Anthony." I stare at her, not really sure if I heard her right.

"What do you mean?" Shadow appears very confused, but determined, like she knows that something needs to be done, but isn't quite sure why.

"Yesterday, when talking about his grandfather, it didn't make sense. If Matteo had been out of the portal he created for this long, I would have sensed the medal's presence. I only started feeling something unusual only a few months ago. Something about his story does not seem true. Watch out for him, I think he is lying to you." I don't have time to ask her anything else since I see the bus approaching. Quickly grabbing my bag, Shadow flies into my medal hidden beneath my jacket, and I run outside to get on the bus.

I make it to the bus just in time and I am sad to see that my usual spot sitting next to Colomba is already taken by Anthony. I sigh to myself as I make my way through the bus aisle and sit in the seat behind them with Nat. It is an annoying ride to say the least.

We make it to school without any issues, and my first few classes go by quickly. It isn't until my second to last class that things go very wrong for me. This is a class I share with Colomba and I didn't really speak with her at all before class started, too wrapped up in my own thoughts to really want to say anything. When the bell rings to signal the end of class, I quickly walk out of the classroom, not wanting to talk to anybody, but Colomba manages to catch up to me easily in the crowded hallway.

"Hey Luis, wait a second." She starts walking beside me, a bit of annoyance and sadness on her face. "Luis, what is wrong? Seriously, you have been acting weird for weeks now and you barely hang out with me anymore. What is up with you? Why are you acting like a jerk?" Without thinking, I turn around to face her, letting out the frustration I have been feeling for what feels like forever.

"You want to know what's wrong? I'll tell you. You and that guy have been bothering me." Her kind and gentle face suddenly changes to show controlled anger as her eyes narrow as she glares at me.

"And by "that guy" I'm guessing you're talking about Anthony." I feel my hands clench into fists at my side.

"Yes, of course I'm talking about Anthony! I don't trust that guy, and yet you are trusting him completely even though we have just met him. And you are acting all mushy around him like you are into him or something!" Colomba crosses her arms in front of her.

"And what if I am interested in him?" All the anger leaves me as it feels like an arrow has gone right through my heart.

"You couldn't possibly love him. You have to trust me when I say that he is bad news." Colomba rolls her eyes at me.

"Oh, c'mon Luis, what evidence do you have for that?" I pause for a moment, knowing that she's right. I don't really have any evidence that he is a bad guy. I just don't like him, and I don't like how he acts with Colomba. I could mention what Shadow had told me, but she would just say it was a guess on Shadow's part, and it doesn't mean anything. Colomba notices my silence and scoffs at me.

"I thought so. You just don't like him, don't you? What do you even have against this guy? I mean, he's always nice to you even though you act like a jerk to him. What is wrong with you? Can't you see that you're being the bad guy here?!" I stay silent, just staring down at my shoes, knowing that I have nothing that I can say to that. My silence seems to just make her more angry since she says softly,

"Well, I guess you have a hard time seeing that you're the bad guy since it took you three years to figure that out with your previous plan as the Crow." I look back up at her, shocked that she would say something like that to me. I look her right in the eyes as I finally find my words.

"That was really messed up for you to say." She doesn't look guilty or apologize, she just states something that sends ice down my spine and puts a hole in my heart.

"No Luis, what's messed up is what you did to me for those three years with everything you did with your powers, and now pulling this stunt with someone who has just joined our team. That is what's really messed up." I don't have any time to think of a response to this since I hear something coming from behind me. Turning around, I can see that it is Anthony. He walks over to us with a friendly smile on his face.

"Hey guys, how are you?" The smile fades when he sees the serious expressions on our faces and feels the tense vibe between us. "Is everything okay?" Colomba lets out a sigh as she walks past me to go towards Anthony.

"Yeah, we are fine. Luis was just leaving though." I look at her, the pain in my heart is stronger, more painful than anything I have ever felt. I can't even move I am so stunned. Colomba is glaring at me right now, and I understand what she is trying to tell me. She wants me to leave now. How could she do this to me? After everything we have gone through together as friends, how could she choose him over me?

When I see Anthony wrap his arm protectively around Colomba, and she leans against him, I know that I can't argue anymore. I have lost today. Anthony is looking down at her with concern; he may not know what happened between Colomba and I, but he is trying to support her anyway. I know that if practically any other guy wrapped his arm around her like that, she would stand up for herself and never let it happen again. She is letting Anthony do it though, she actually seems to like it.

Turning around, I walk off to head to my final class of the day. Hopefully tomorrow I can talk to her. I will not be in school tomorrow since my uncle scheduled a doctor's appointment and a dentist appointment in the same day, but hopefully after school when we meet up for training, I can speak to her before Anthony shows up. I don't want her to stay mad at me. I want to make things better between us. Even if she may have feelings for him now, I still don't want her to hate me. I will always love her, and I won't let one argument ruin things for us. I will just give us both some time to cool off, and by this time tomorrow I'm sure everything will be just fine. It has to be.

My next class is art. Mr. Sizemore tells us that we can spend this class to work on our current projects. I get my supplies out and silently get to work. My heart hurts a bit now when I look at my project. I had started on a portrait of Silver Dove, I wanted to give it to Colomba since I have been upsetting her recently with how I've been acting. I guess I can't really do that anymore, she wouldn't accept it if I tried to give it to her now. I silently look down at it, feeling my heart ripping itself apart looking at it. In this picture, I made her look as perfect as she looks to me, but she would never accept that. She only has eyes for Anthony and has obviously chosen him over me, it doesn't even feel like she wants me as a friend anymore. As I sit here feeling sorry for myself, someone seems to have noticed my misery.

"Hello Luis, is something bothering you today?" I look up at Mr. Sizemore, who is looking at me with concern. Like a parent looking at a crying child.

"What makes you say that?" I respond with, which only makes him chuckle, as if the answer to my question is obvious.

"Well, usually you get started on your projects right away instead of staring at it like your world is coming apart. So, tell me, what's wrong?" I look up at Mr. Sizemore's kind face, and I know that I can't hide anything from him, so it's better if I just tell him the truth.

"Do you remember Colomba, the girl that I did the portrait of for that contest at the county fair?" Mr. Sizemore smiles and nods at this.

"Yes, I remember, it was a lovely portrait of a lovely young lady." I sigh, thinking about how happy the two of us were together at that point. It hurts my heart now to think about it.

"Yeah, well I've liked her for ages, but she seems interested in someone else now, and I don't know what to do." Mr. Sizemore appears thoughtful for a moment before he asks me a weird question.

"Tell me, have you ever told her how you feel?" I shake my head. "Is she already with this other person?" I shake my head again. "Well then it seems like you still have a chance." I lower my head, shaking it again, feeling disappointed.

"Not really, she would never say yes to me." Mr. Sizemore sits down on the table in front of me, looking down at me as if he is the one disappointed in me.

"Luis, on that day at the fair, I could tell that you both had very positive feelings towards each other. There might be something there. All you can really do is either tell her how you feel or regret it later when she does eventually go out with someone else." I will admit, it hurts my heart a little having him say almost the exact same thing several other people have told me. When I don't say anything back to him, Mr. Sizemore continues to speak. "You can't expect her to come up to you and express how she feels, especially if she is starting to feel some way about someone else. You will need to explain how you feel or else she will never know. I saw how you two were around each other, there is a chance for you, I'm sure of it." Without another word, Mr. Sizemore leaves me alone with my thoughts.

As I look down at my picture of Silver Dove again, I can't help but realize that everyone has been right all along. I can't keep pushing this off. I need to tell her how I feel before anything else happens. I can't lose her. I can't let her start hating me because of how I have been lately. I need to just explain that I am jealous of Anthony and that I want to be with her.

She might turn me down... Who am I kidding? She will probably turn me down, I mean she's pretty amazing and I'm a less than ordinary guy, she deserves better than me, but I have to try. Since the school day is ending, and I will be absent tomorrow because of my appointments, I will try to speak with her after school tomorrow. I can't just speak through her mind with the power of our medals since I want to do it face to face. I want her to see that I am being truthful with her. I don't want to be a coward anymore.

Picking up my pencil, I start working on my portrait of Silver Dove again, feeling hope in my chest. Things might actually be okay.

Chapter Eleven

Colomba-
I Don't Know
What To Do

Today is starting off a bit strange. First off, my dad is driving me to school instead of me taking the bus like usual. I think he could see how upset I was yesterday and wanted some private time with me this morning to talk about it, since he kept asking me if everything is okay as we drove. I tried to explain to him that everything is fine, but I'm sure he could tell that is a lie. I just didn't want to tell him that one of my friends is acting like a jerk since a new guy has joined our little group of superheroes. I don't think he would understand that.

And second, Luis won't be at school today. Luis is one of those people that never misses school. Like in the few years we have gone to school together, I don't think he has ever missed a day. It will feel weird not being able to see him throughout the day. Thankfully, Nat and Anthony will still be here. I really need them in my life right now with how badly

Luis has been. I need their positive vibes, lately Luis just brings me down.

My first few classes went by smoothly, and now I can finally have lunch with Anthony and Nat. When I arrive in the cafeteria with my packed lunch, I look over to the table we usually sit at to see that Anthony is the only one there right now. Nat is probably still in line to get food. I sit down beside Anthony, trying to smile at him cheerfully, but from the concern on his face I can tell that he can see the pain I feel on the inside.

"Hello Colomba, are you feeling alright?" I shrug at him, knowing that I can't hide from him, and I don't really want to either. I feel like I could tell him everything and he will actually care about what I have to say. I never want to hide anything from him.

"Not really, I'm just worried about how Luis has been acting recently. It feels like it's more than just him being upset because of you joining us. He seems really angry with the two of us. I just don't want to lose any of my friends because of some silly argument." Anthony nods at this. A thoughtful look comes across his face, and he cautiously looks over at me, as if nervous about what he has to say.

"Do you think that it is because he is jealous of us?" I look at Anthony, not really understanding what he means. Anthony seems to notice my confusion since he explains. "Well, it seems that he really likes you, and we have been getting pretty close and he has been avoiding us when we are together. Do you think that he is jealous because he really likes you and he doesn't like me being around you?" I lower my gaze from his, knowing that he is right, but I don't want him to be right. I want Luis to be angry for a different reason. Having it be like this only makes things more confusing. I don't want so much emotion tied into this, so we can more easily solve all this. I want us to all just get along. I let out a soft sigh before I finally say what needs to be said.

"Yeah, you're right. He is jealous. Luis wants things to be like they were before you arrived, when we figured out who each other is and started working together. He wants it to just be us again, but we can't go backwards with this. I want you on our team, you are meant to work with us, but Luis doesn't see it that way." I close my eyes, feeling a headache coming along thanks to how frustrated I feel right now. I open my eyes in shock when I feel someone place their hand gently on top of mine. Looking down, I can see that Anthony is smiling softly at me, his hand holding mine. He is looking into my eyes as if everything is right with the world despite what I just told him.

"I can understand why he would be jealous. I think practically everyone would be jealous of us." Slowly lifting my hand to his lips, he kisses it like an old school gentleman before he smiles at me. I can't help it, I melt, I melt all over the floor at the sight of that smile. I smile back at him, and for a moment, neither of us speaks, we just look into each other's eyes, and everything feels perfect in those few seconds. Of course, something has to ruin it.

A loud crashing comes from somewhere across the room, followed by many people starting to scream. Anthony and I look away from each other to see something that makes my heart sink into my chest and the world seems to freeze around me as terror fills my soul.

Standing on top of the broken fragments of the window it had obviously jumped through is one of the Crow's shadow dogs. This one seems much larger than usual. The shadow dog is almost as tall as a horse, it has its head lowered as it growls at the people around it. Everyone scatters at the sight of this thing as more of these demonic dogs leap through the broken window. Outside, I can see more of these things running around, entering the school through other windows. I can hear people in the other rooms these dogs are entering screaming in fear as I see a huge crowd running through the hallway.

One of the dogs that had come in through the window turns and faces Anthony and me. My eyes grow wide in horror as it slowly moves closer to us, keeping its head low like it is a predator stalking its prey. I feel my heart pounding in my chest, but I can't move, my mind is racing too fast for me to even recognize that I am in danger.

What is going on? Why did the Crow- Why did *Luis* make these things? And why is he making these things attack the school? What is going on right now?

I am snapped out of my thoughts by someone grabbing my hand and yanking me out of my seat right before the shadow dog leaped at us, now crashing into the chairs we had just been sitting in seconds ago. I start running, seeing that the person holding my hand and leading me through the halls in Anthony. As we run, all around us is chaos. Everyone is screaming, they are all trying to outrun each other, trying to move faster so that they won't be caught by these creatures. Some of the slower people in the crowd are crying as the shadow dogs nip at the ankles as they desperately try to run faster.

With Anthony leading me, we outrun everyone, turn down a hallway, and quickly slip into a janitor's closet. He closes the door quickly, keeping his ear on the door to see if anybody is coming our way. With the silence I hear, I'm guessing nobody is there. When he is sure that we are safe, he turns to me, worry in his eyes. He holds my shoulders gently, trying to comfort me, looking into my eyes, I feel a bit better already just knowing that I am here with him.

"Colomba, are you alright?" Even though I don't feel emotionally alright, I'm pretty sure he's talking about did I get hurt, so I nod my head.

"Yes, I'm alright, but what is going on? Why are there the shadow dogs all around us? Luis isn't even supposed to be at school today; why is he doing this?" Anthony lowers his gaze from mine. He lets out a little sigh before he answers me.

"He must be done with his appointments and decided to come to school to get some revenge." I feel my body stiffen in fear.

"Revenge? What are you talking about? Why would Luis want to do this?" Anthony looks back up at me, a deep sadness in his eyes.

"You said earlier that Luis was upset, and he seems to be upset about us. It seems like he is trying to get revenge against us. Based on what he has done before with his powers, he doesn't really seem like a stable guy. This is probably his way of getting revenge against us." I feel my eyes grow wide and my heart starts to pound as panic fills me.

"No, no he wouldn't do that, he wouldn't do that to us." My voice sounds unsure, like I am trying to lie to myself. Even though I can feel these lies, I keep lying to myself. "He wouldn't hurt all these people just because he is jealous of us. He wouldn't do that." Anthony is looking down at me with pity in his eyes. He pulls me in close to hug my, keeping me close to his chest as the lies keep escaping my lips. "He promised that he wouldn't do stuff like this anymore. He promised, he wouldn't lie to me. He wouldn't do that, he's one of my best friends." Anthony puts his hand under my chin, lifting it so that I am looking in his eyes.

"He lied to all of us. He did all the damage as the Crow all these years because he was mad and in pain, and now he's doing it again because he is mad about us. We cannot change what he has done, but we can try to stop him." Taking in a deep breath, I nod, knowing that Anthony is right. We have been betrayed, and we have to do whatever we can to stop him.

Without saying another word to each other, the two of us close our eyes, and even through my closed eyes, I can still see the blinding light as we both transform. When the light has disappeared, I open my eyes to see a knight in golden armor in front of me. The two of us look at each other, our massive wings crowding the already tiny janitor's closet. We both nod at each other before Anthony turns around and opens the door, chaos is all around us, but we are ready.

As soon as we leave the closet, we have our weapons ready. Anthony as Golden Eagle has his bow drawn while I have my sword held up, ready to strike. Near me, a shadow dog is slowly creeping closer to a girl who is cowering in a corner, too scared to move. Rushing over, I swipe my sword at it when it is only inches away from the girl. The shadow dog disappears as my sword goes right through it. Behind me, Golden Eagle releases one golden arrow after another, each one hitting their targets, making at least ten shadow dogs disappear in seconds. As I take a moment to watch him, he releases an arrow at a shadow dog who is dragging someone by the hood of their jacket. Golden Eagle hit the dog right in the head, only inches from hitting the student as well. As soon as the shadow dog disappeared, the student was able to get up and run away. Wow this guy is really impressive to make a shot like that.

The two of us look at each other, and immediately I know what he is thinking. This hallway is clear now, we need to go to the next. I nod at him and the two of us fly down the hallway together as the people we just rescued cheer for us as we leave them behind. As soon as we turn into the next hall, we are greeted by the sight of at least thirty shadow dogs using their teeth to rip apart papers as well as lockers. Some are cornering students as if they are trying to keep them prisoner while others howl in victory, creating a sound that echoes down the hall that sends shivers down my spine. Something about the shadow dogs seems more vicious than usual. Before, Luis would only make the dogs cause a bit of chaos, now though, they are doing some serious damage. The dogs are practically ripping apart the school with their teeth. I watch as one grips a locker door with its teeth and throws it at a window, shattering it, showering broken glass on top of several students cowering beneath the window.

Golden Eagle lets an arrow fly, hitting one of the shadow dogs right between its glowing red eyes, making it disappear like the shadow it is. With one of them gone, the others turn to face us, growling furiously at the loss of one of their friends. I lift my sword as they all rush at us, swinging it right at the face of the demon dog leading the charge. I don't stop swinging, I can't stop. They keep coming as soon as one is defeated another seems to come out of nowhere to take its place. As I thrust my sword into the neck of a shadow dog, I hear someone shout my name. Quickly turning around, I am face to face with a shadow dog, its mouth wide open, about to snap my head in its jaws. When its fangs are only inches from my skin, the beast disappears as Golden Eagle swings his bow right through it. With that one gone, we are now alone in the hallway. He looks down at me with concern in his eyes.

"Are you alright, Silver Dove?" I nod.

"Yes, I'm alright." Golden Eagle nods back.

"Good, because I think we have a bit more fighting to do." Golden Eagle points down the hall, I turn around to see a crowd of the shadow dogs running right towards us. All of them barking and howling in rage at seeing their enemies. Golden Eagle and I look at each other for only a moment before we face the angry beasts again.

The next twenty minutes is just a blur of sword slashing and Golden Eagle's arrows flying through the air. Countless shadow dogs disappear around us until we are the only ones left. The two of us look around to see that there aren't any of the dogs left. When we are sure that the chaos is over, I use my powers to clean up the mess that the shadow dogs created, making it look like nothing ever happened.

As Anthony and I look around to see that the school is back to normal, we smile at each other, but we are not able to celebrate since the bell rings and the principal comes over the intercom to tell everyone that they can leave for the day now that the shadow dogs have been destroyed. Golden Eagle and I fly through the hallways as everyone starts leaving their classrooms.

As we fly towards the front doors, I hear countless people talking to their friends about what just happened, wondering why it happened. They ask each other why the Crow did this, how Golden Eagle and I let this happen, and what caused the Crow to become the bad guy again. When we are almost out the door, someone actually yells out to me, venom in their voice, "Silver Dove, you told us we could trust him now! Why did you lie to us?!" I don't stop to answer that question, mostly because I don't have an answer. I just fly by them with Golden Eagle by my side. The two of us head to the field where the three of us have been training together. Hopefully Luis will show up there so we can get an explanation, but I doubt it. He would have to be a real idiot to show up today with how angry I feel towards him right now.

Chapter Twelve

Luis-
The Horrible
Lie

With all appointments done, I fly over the town to head to the field where Colomba, Anthony, and I have been training together after school. The school day just ended about forty minutes ago so they should be there by now. My heart is pounding in my chest and my stomach is tying itself into knots.

I'm going to do it. As soon as training is over, I'm going to get Colomba alone and I'm going to tell her how I really feel. The wind blows against my face as I fly over farmland, but I am still sweating in my anxiety. I've held this secret inside for so long, and now I am finally going to tell her that I love her. When I think about Anthony though, I can't help but wonder if this will all be for nothing. She may love him instead of me, but I've got to try. It only takes another minute or so to make it to the training field. I can see that Colomba and Anthony are already there.

Flying above them, I see Colomba sitting on a large rock with Anthony standing beside her, his hand resting on her shoulder. It almost looks like he is trying to comfort her, but that can't be right, what could he be comforting her about. Did something bad happen today? I have to make sure that she is alright.

I let myself glide down to the ground, landing gently as I transform back into my regular self. When they hear me land, Colomba and Anthony look at me at first with surprise, and then that changes into something that I'm not really sure what it is. I walk over to them and Colomba gets off the rock she was sitting on and almost marches towards me with determination. There is something dark in her perfect aquamarine eyes. Did something bad happen to upset her today, what's going on?

"Hey guys what's-" My question is interrupted as Colomba reaches her hand back and slaps me across the face with so much force that I almost fall down. I'm able to catch myself at the last second to keep myself standing as I turn to face Colomba, seeing her cheeks red in rage and her eyes burning with what looks like hatred. I am in so much pain from her strike, but I ignore it to keep all my attention on her. I feel my heart shattering at the sight of that hatred. What is going on? Why is she looking at me like that? Why is she looking at me like I am her enemy?

"Colomba, why-" She doesn't even let me finish my question.

"How could you do this after all we have gone through together?!" Her voice is cold and harsh, but beneath the strong mask she's wearing, I can hear the pain and hurt she is trying to hide from me. My face stings from her slap, but I don't even care about that, all I notice are the tears forming in her eyes.

"What are you talking about, Colomba? I didn't-" Anthony steps forward, getting in between me and Colomba while Colomba takes a few steps away, turning away from me as if she doesn't even want to look at me.

"Don't even talk to her, you creep, we know what you did." Anthony looks at me as if he is looking at a disgusting bug. I ignore him though; he doesn't matter to me. All that matters to me right now is Colomba.

"Colomba, please just tell me what I did. I don't understand what's going on." Colomba turns back around to reveal the tears of misery falling down her face.

"How could you not know what you did?! You sent a bunch of your shadow dogs to the school and wrecked everything! You could have hurt someone! You almost hurt me!" The betrayal in her voice stabs me in the chest, sending ice through my veins. What is she talking about? How could my shadow dogs have been at the school? I wasn't even there. Plus, why would I do this? Why would I want to hurt Colomba or anybody else? I have changed my ways, I am not like how I was last year. I don't want to be that person again.

I try to move closer to her, but Anthony holds his arm out, blocking me from her. Anthony glares at me like a protective dog guarding their owner. I look past him to stare at Colomba, my stomach turning over on itself as I see the tears rolling down her cheeks.

"Colomba, I don't know what happened today, but I promise you that it wasn't me. I wasn't even near the school all day." I feel the tears beginning to sting in my eyes as I see the disbelief in her gaze. "Please, you've got to believe me. I wouldn't do this." Anthony just scoffs at this.

"And why should we believe you? You were always doing stuff like this just last year. What makes now so different?" I want to punch Anthony in the face so bad right now, but I know that will just make things worse for me. Instead, I look him in the eyes as I respond.

"Because I have changed, that's why." I turn my attention back to Colomba, but she looks down at her feet as soon as our eyes meet, almost as if she is afraid that she will start believing me if she looks into my eyes. "Colomba, you have seen how much I have changed since then. I have worked so hard to get where I am now. Why would I go back on all of that just to attack people? What would I get from all that?" Colomba's mask of misery changes to an expression of confusion, as if she is really thinking about what I am saying, but Anthony once again interrupts me.

"Maybe you did it because you were upset. Let's face it, you aren't really the kind of guy who can control his emotions." I want to hit him so bad, I am practically shaking trying to hold in my anger right now. I can't hit him that will only prove him right. All I can do is just stand here as he keeps growling his words at me. "It seems that whenever you got upset about something, the Crow would suddenly pop up and cause chaos, am I right?" I stay silent, a part of me upset with myself since I know he is right. I mean, the first time I showed myself as the Crow it was because Alex was about to ask Colomba on a date and I didn't want that to happen. I couldn't let him get too close to her. At the time, it felt like the right thing to do. Now though, I just feel like an idiot. I glare at him, doing everything I can to try and sound calm when I really just want to scream at him.

"I was at some doctor's appointments today, I wasn't near the school. It wasn't me." Anthony just chuckles and shakes his head, like I am being stupid.

"And why should we believe that? You could have had your appointments and then gone to the school afterwards, you may not have had any appointments at all. They were your shadow dogs, it's not like just anybody can create those things. Face it Luis, you got caught red handed. You were really stupid to think you could get away with something like this using your powers." Once again, I look past him to see Colomba. She has her back turned to me, but from how her body is shaking, I know that she is crying.

"Colomba, please-"

"Just go, Luis." Her voice is weak and full of betrayal and misery. I try to walk towards her, to try and comfort her, but Anthony puts his hand on my chest, stopping me.

"You should do what she said and leave, you've caused enough damage today." Just from his tone, I can tell that I am not going to get any closer to her without a fight. And from how she sounded just a moment ago, I know that there is nothing I can say to make this better. All I can do is leave.

I turn away from them, feeling as if I am walking away from everything. When I am a few feet away, I look back to see that Anthony has his arm around her in a gentle, comforting hug as he whispers soft words to her. When he notices me looking at them, a cold, victorious smile crawls across his face, an evil expression I have never seen on his face before. My blood chills at the sight of it, and I instantly know what really happened. As Golden Eagle, he can create whatever he imagines, so he imagined a bunch of my shadow dogs to attack the school and make it look like I did it. But why? Why would he do this to me?

As I watch that smile instantly disappear to become a look of concern and comfort as he begins to speak soft words to Colomba again, I know my answer. He did this to get me out of the way to get closer to her. As I watch, she turns to face Anthony, burying her sobbing face into his chest as he holds her tightly against himself. Just from seeing that, I know that I can't say anything right now, she trusts him too much while she sees me as the enemy. I need to wait.

Transforming into the Crow again, I spread out my wings and begin to fly away. The sounds of Colomba sobbing in betrayal haunting my mind as tears start falling down my face as well. I worked so hard to change myself to be a better person, so that I won't be hurt or hurt others anymore, and someone still makes sure that I have to suffer. No matter what I do, I lose. After all of this, how can I ever convince Colomba that I didn't do anything wrong? That I am not a monster? How can I do that when she obviously believes whatever Anthony has told her? Why did it all have to end like this? Why do I always have to be the loser no matter whether I'm on the good or bad side?

These questions keep swirling through my mind as I fly through the air, the tears drip off of my face and fall down to the earth below probably feeling like raindrops to everyone beneath me.

Chapter Thirteen

Colomba-
My Breaking
Heart

Anthony holds onto me tightly as I cry. My heart feels as if it being torn apart in my chest. How could my best friend betray me like this? Even before we knew who each other were, he was never so brutal with his demon dogs. Why would he act out like this now? Was Anthony right, and he's just jealous that Anthony is now part of our team and is getting more positive attention than him? Would Luis really care that much about the attention? I can't think right with all these questions running through my mind, but having Anthony hold me does make everything feel a little bit better. I feel so safe in his arms, as if I will always be safe and that I can truly trust him.

I can't believe I had let myself believe that Luis had changed. I mean, he had acted as the villain for about three years and then suddenly changed? I had to have been so stupid to think he could change that much in so little time. I guess I just hoped that my friend would be better than that, that I could trust this guy who had helped me so much in my life. I guess that some people just don't change, they let the anger in their heart control them.

I can only hope that he won't try to fight back against us because we probably just made him a whole lot angrier with what just happened. I mean, I did just slap him in my anger, and it looked like I really hurt his feelings; would he try to strike back against us? Would he really want to hurt me after all our years of friendship? Did our friendship really mean nothing to him that he would throw it all away to get back at us just because I was friends with another guy? Did I really lose a friend just because of this?

I don't need to let that worry me though, as long as I have Anthony by my side, I'm sure we can get through anything together. I can only hope that we won't have to fight against Luis. I'm not sure I could fight against him again since I would know who he really is. How can I fight someone who is my best friend… well I guess I should say he was my best friend. I can't be friends with someone who would do this. After all we have gone through together, I guess it's all over now, this was the last straw. I won't let myself be friends with someone who hurts and betrays me like this. I let myself get pushed around for a while with Alex always trying to push my boundaries and try to get closer to me, I won't let Luis do the same. I won't be friends with someone who doesn't deserve my time. After what he did today, he does not deserve my time, or anything from me.

For now, I just need to learn to live without him. I know that it will be hard since we have helped each other grow and have been so close for so long, but I know now that I am strong enough to do this. He has been my friend for so long, but I am sure that Anthony will help heal my broken heart. I know that Anthony is a good guy, he will help me heal. Right now he is telling me that everything will be alright, and that he will stay by my side, that he won't let Luis hurt me. I let myself relax in his arms, letting Anthony hold me tight. I know he is telling me the truth. I am safe with him, he would never hurt me. Unlike Luis, Anthony would never betray me. I stay in Anthony's arms, happy to be held by him, feeling a little bit of joy in this dark moment, knowing that I have someone with me that I can trust, someone who truly cares about me.

It feels as if he holds on to me for ages, comforting me, but it was probably only a few minutes. We talk for a little while longer, him mostly making sure that I am really alright, before he flies me home. He insisting on taking me home since he was scared that Luis might try to do something to me if I was alone. It was so kind of him to do that. It's frightening to think about what Luis could do to me if Anthony wasn't there.

As soon as I get inside, I am looking for Nonna. She had been running errands when I had gotten home from school earlier, so I haven't been able to tell her what had happened. I find her in the sewing room, working on a new dress for me. She glances up from her work with a cheerful smile on her face.

"Oh hello, Tesoro. I'm glad you're here. I need you to try this dress on to make sure it fits right." I shake my head, a little upset with myself, knowing that I will be spoiling her good mood.

"Maybe later, right now I have to tell you something, something really important." Nonna sets the dress back down, her eyes narrowing with confusion.

"What's wrong, Tesoro? Did something happen today?" I nod, taking in a deep breath before I explain the tragedy that happened today. She sits there silently as I speak about what happened at school as well as what happened in the field only a little bit ago, her face an emotionless mask that I can't read.

"So, Luis is no longer my friend, and he's back to being an enemy again. Thankfully I now have Anthony to help me fight him. I just can't believe that he would do this to me, after everything we have gone through together. I know that he has been kinda drifting away from me for a while since he was jealous, but I never thought that he would do something like this." Nonna nods at this, her eyes thoughtful as I pace back and forth across the room. I'm too agitated right now to be able to sit still.

"Yes, I don't believe it either. Something seems very wrong here." I can't help but scoff at that.

"Yeah, and the thing that's wrong is Luis. I can't believe he would try to hurt so many people just because he was jealous. How pathetic can you be?" I look down at the Silver Dove Pin on my cardigan, my heart breaking a little more thinking about all that I have done and sacrificed as Silver Dove just for things to end out like this. "I guess we shouldn't be surprised though, based on how Luis was using his powers before all this. The guy was giving people powers so that they could get revenge, we should have expected this from him. The guy has no control over his emotions." Nonna lets out a little sigh, taking my hands and silently leading me to a chair to sit down beside her. She takes a moment before speaking, resting her hands on mine, a sad smile on her face.

"People do strange things when they are in love." She squeezes my hand softly as she tries to hold back tears. "I have been able to see this for a long time, and I've told you this before, but I don't think you truly believed me. Luis loves you so much. I think he even gave up his plan as the Crow because he realized you were Silver Dove. He was willing to give up a plan he had since he started high school, and he kept it up for three years, but he gave it up for you. I've seen how he looks at you, he would do anything for you. He only did this because he could see how you were getting close to Anthony, he was afraid he was loosing you." My eyes open wide in shock at her words.

"That's not an excuse for his behavior! Just because he's jealous doesn't mean that I should forgive him for what he did today. He hurt a lot of people, and I won't let him be my friend anymore if he does that instead of just moving on. Luis should respect how I feel inside of lashing out at everyone else because he doesn't like how things are turning out for himself." Nonna looks at me, surprised by how by how harshly I'm speaking about him.

"But Tesoro, he's your best friend." Her words almost come out as a whisper, I can't help but look down at my hands, not wanting to see the pain in her eyes.

"Yeah, not anymore though. He's not my best friend, and he's not even a friend at this point. Luis has not only burned that bridge, he has just completely wrecked it. I never want to see him again." Nonna lowers her head, she can probably tell from my voice that I am not going to back down with this, no matter what she says.

"How can you do that though, you both go to the same school. Luis will try to talk with you again. What will you do when he does that?" A shiver goes through my whole body at the thought of that happening. A dark cloud seems to hang over me as I think about what could happen if he tries to talk to me. What would I do? Would I just run away from him, or would I try speaking with him? I look back up to look Nonna in the eyes when I give her my honest answer.

"I don't know what I will do. I guess I'll just figure that out when I get there. All I know is that I won't let him back into my life again. I already gave him a chance to still be my friend after I found out that he was the Crow, I won't make that mistake again." The dark cloud seems to clear up a bit as a bright thought enters my mind and a small smile comes across my face. "But I have Anthony now, and he can help me with this. I won't be alone in my fight anymore." Nonna gives me a sad little smile.

"Yes, I'm sure he would be happy to protect you from anything. He seems to care for you a lot." I feel my face grow warm, and I know that I must be as red as a tomato.

"Yeah, I think he would. I know that I will be safe with him no matter what." She nods at this, still trying to smile even though I can see the disappointment in her eyes. I have had the feeling for a while that she wanted Luis and I to start dating, that she thought we would be a good couple. Seeing me go for another guy, who is the grandson of one of the enemies she had when she was Silver Dove is probably not a very comforting thought for her. Something in my gut tells me that she still doesn't fully trust Anthony because of what his grandfather did, but I'm sure that she just needs to spend more time with him and then she will like him. Maybe she will even approve of Anthony and I dating, it would be the best day of my life if she would approve of that.

Chapter Fourteen

Luis-
Confusion and
Pain

I sit on my bed, not moving, not sure of what I can do. I feel like I am a zombie, dead but still stuck here on earth. My entire body feels heavy and worn out even though I'm not tired. More than anything right now, I wish that I didn't exist. I wish I could just melt into the floor, then I wouldn't have to deal with how I am feeling right now.

I just got back from the training clearing a few minutes ago, and I am back in my regular form while Shadow just stares at me while perched on the back of a chair, almost like she is waiting for me to say something, but I don't know what to say.

I bury my face in my hands so that I won't have to look at her. I can't stand seeing her black eyes on me. I want to be alone, but I know that I can never escape Shadow, she is always with me even when I can't see her, whether I like it or not.

Why is this happening to me? I thought that when I stopped doing all the crazy stuff I was doing before as the Crow that things would finally work out for me. I would get closer to Colomba and we could possibly start dating, I thought that I would be happier, and I thought that things would actually be better, that together we could make the world a better place. I was definitely wrong. Things started off great, but as soon as Anthony showed up, everything changed. She started hanging out more with him, he started getting in between us, and I sort of, well maybe just a little… okay maybe a lot, I got super crazy jealous of that and I acted mean because of it. I shouldn't have, I know that, but seeing them together like that just tore me apart, I couldn't stand it. I hated seeing how he made her smile, how she laughed at his jokes, how she let him get so close to her compared to any other guy. Why did he have to show up now? Why couldn't the world just let me be happy for once in my life? Why couldn't I finally have a chance with the girl I have loved for so long? Why do I have to be so pathetic no matter what I do? I fail when I'm the bad guy, I fail when I'm a good guy, why can't the world just let me win for once in my life?

Lifting my head again, I see that Shadow is still staring at me. Her black eyes look straight into mine, waiting, waiting for… I don't know what. I sigh, feeling defeated by her silence.

"Alright, what? What do you want?" Shadow's eyes narrow and I see her feathers fluffing out a bit in her rage.

"I'm waiting." I groan softly, knowing that I will be playing into her trap when I ask her what I know she wants me to say.

"For what?" Shadow suddenly opens up her wings, making me jerk back slightly, almost afraid that she was going to hit me or something.

"*For you to stop feeling sorry for yourself and to get back up!!*" I get close to her, now ready for a fight.

"And what exactly am I supposed to do?! She hates me now! What can I possibly do to make her not hate me?! I would need to prove that I didn't do this, and Anthony did! Problem is she already thinks that I have it out for Anthony and would think I am just blaming him so I could get out of trouble!"

Her fluffed-out feathers slowly lie back down as she takes a deep breath to calm herself. She turns her head to look away from me.

"Honestly, I don't know. This young man seems to have manipulated the situation to fit exactly as he wanted to. He knew how you felt and used that against you and made you appear to be the one being aggressive towards him for no reason. With how you have acted in the past, Colomba wouldn't have been surprised if you did act out in this way." I open my mouth to try and argue with her about that, but I quickly close it when I realize she is telling the truth. I have acted out a lot when I felt angry, I have to admit that about myself at this point, there's no escaping it. Anthony apparently learned a lot about me in the little time he has been with us to be able to make this plan look like it was mine. I sigh, feeling more defeated than I ever have before, even compared to all the times Silver Dove defeated me in the past.

"So, what do we do now? How can I make this

right again? Is that even possible?" Shadow remains silent for a moment, thinking about my questions. After a minute of silence, I start thinking that even an intelligent creature like her won't be able to think of anything, that I truly am hopeless. My heart leaps a little in my chest when she finally lifts her head to look at me again.

"Time. That is what we need." I narrow my eyes with confusion as I look at her.

"What do you mean?"

"It means that we need to be patient." Shadow says with a bit of annoyance in her voice at having to explain a simple idea to me. "Colomba is a very forgiving and kind person, if we let her anger from today die down a little bit over time, she may be willing to listen to what you have to say at that point. When she is calmer, I can try to talk to her as well. If she hears me back up your story, then she might start realizing that you were being honest with her. After that, then we can figure out how to deal with Anthony, this new Golden Eagle." Shadow places her wing beneath her beak, like a person putting their hand under their chin when they are thinking.

"Something tells me that Anthony didn't do this just to get you away from Colomba so that he could get closer to her. There is something far more sinister at play. He has something planned, but I'm not quite sure what it is at this point. We will need to keep our eyes on him." I nod at this, knowing that she is speaking the truth.

Something dark and sinister is coming our way, and what frightens me is that I don't really know what it is. What is Anthony planning? What is he trying to do by doing this to me? What is really going on right now? Something is hidden, and I have a feeling that it is coming for Colomba. Even if she may be against me right now, I need to protect her from whatever this is. I know that she probably hates me right now, but I can live with that if I know that she will be safe. I can let myself live with that for a while if I know that she isn't getting hurt. I need her to be safe and happy, nothing else really matters.

I stare out the window, wondering what will happen now that this has happened. My mind tumbles through many different possibilities of what Anthony might be planning, but none of them truly feel right. I end up giving up on trying to figure it out. Instead, I think about Colomba, hoping and praying that by tomorrow I can try to talk with her, that she won't just run away or scream at me. I feel a horrible pain in my heart at the thought of her running away from me, seeing fear in her eyes when she looks at me. I don't know if my heart can take it if she does that. I don't know if I could survive if she was afraid of me.

I watch all the people returning to their homes and closing up their shops in the downtown street beneath me. I can't help but wonder about what their lives must be like, and I wonder if they are as miserable as I feel right now.

Chapter Fifteen

Colomba-
The Next Day

All around me, people are running around and laughing with their friends, eager to start a new day of school while I feel like the world is crumbling around me. I want to join in their happiness, but I don't know when I will be able to feel truly happy again.

I had asked my dad this morning if he could drive me to school instead of taking the bus. He could somehow tell that I was upset by something, and was kind enough to not ask why. I don't know if I could have told him that I was trying to avoid Luis on the bus. I don't know what I could have told him if he did ask me about it. How could I have possibly explained to him that the guy who had been my best friend yesterday is now one of my worst enemies? I don't think I could have come up with something believable to answer that question. It's not like I could tell my dad that Luis is the Crow and is once again trying to cause chaos at my school. If I did tell my dad that, then Luis would just get hurt, and then he would expose me as Silver Dove and Anthony as Golden Eagle. Nobody would win if I did that, so I just have to stay silent.

I can't believe I trusted him. I mean, I have been fighting Luis as the Crow ever since we started high school together; why did I think I could trust him now after all that? Why did I have to be so stupid and trusting? I shake my head, knowing the answer to that question. I trusted him because I wanted to believe that he could change. I wanted to think that he could be a better person. After all the pain he has caused, I should have known that I was wrong. I just couldn't let myself believe that the shy, sweet friend I had known this whole time could be a monster.

I was wrong though, he is a monster.

Luis has caused everyone in this school so much stress and misery, including me, especially me. I had to fight him constantly, and have to deal with all the craziness as Silver Dove. My heart stops for a moment when another thought hits me. I also had to deal with his craziness as my regular self. When he was the Crow, he told me how much he cares about me. That caused me more stress than anything I have ever had in my life. If he loves me as much as he says, then how could he have done this to me? To love someone means that you will never hurt them, and you do your best to try and make them happy; Luis did the opposite. He caused me pain with every opportunity he had with his powers. Luis may not have realized who I really was before, but now he does, yet he still did that yesterday. He is the monster that everyone has always said he is.

Right now, a few members of his fan club are walking beside me, and even they are complaining about what he did. They're saying that he was finally getting on everyone's good side and was making things better, and then he had to ruin it by attacking everyone for no reason. He's even lost their love.

I can hear other voices though, whispering things to each other that puts a rock in the pit of my stomach. All around me, people are pretty much repeating exactly what I have been telling myself ever since the attack yesterday. Everyone is calling me an idiot for thinking that the Crow could change so quickly, and that everything that happened yesterday is my fault. That all of their pain and fear was caused by me. Many of them are wondering if this is the start of the Crow doing all his craziness again. That he will continue to transform people like he did before, and I can't help but wonder the same thing. Will all of this start all over again? And will it be worse than before since he now knows who I am?

My pounding heart starts to calm down when I realize the obvious. I won't be alone this time. Even though Luis may try to do something to me again, I have Anthony now. As Golden Eagle he can help me protect the school, he can help protect me. I don't have to be afraid if I have him by my side. No matter what, I know that Anthony will stay by my side. I feel as if a weight has been lifted off of me when I think about Anthony, everything will be fine if I have him by my side.

As I turn a corner to go down a different hallway, I glance through the crowd of people and I see a familiar face that sends ice down my spine. Luis is walking down the hall, heading towards me with his head hanging, like he is having a terrible day even though the day has just started.

He looks up when someone bumps into him, and his eyes land on me. A spark of hope and joy lights up his face as he starts coming towards me. I should run, I know I should run, but something keeps my feet glued to the ground. Fear. For the first time in my life, I am too afraid to even move. Usually, whenever I have been truly afraid of something, I knew I needed to fight it, to fight back against whatever it is, when I look at Luis though I don't feel that way. Despite everything he has done, I cannot bring myself to fight him. It is so strange to know that the fear I feel is coming from a person who was my best friend just two days ago. What am I going to do? He's too close now for me to run, with his speed he could easily catch up to me. What is he going to do? What am I going to do?

All the terror leaves me as I feel a strong arm wrap around my shoulders. Looking to my side, I see Anthony smiling comfortingly at me for a moment before lifting his gaze to glare at Luis who is now only about six feet away. The two silently glare at each other, as if challenging the other to say something. Daring the other to do something.

The three of us stand in silence, nobody moving, until the bell rings, warning us that we only have one more minute to get to class. Anthony and Luis give each other one final burning glare before Anthony just smirks slightly and scoffs before letting his eyes leave Luis to look back down at me. His arm around my shoulders, pulls me in closer into a gentle embrace. This seems to make Luis bristle a bit in anger, but he still doesn't move closer to us. Luis just looks at me pitifully, as if he is hoping that I will walk away from Anthony and go to him instead. Luis must be very disappointed when I turn my head to ignore him, and instead look up at Anthony.

I glance up to see Anthony's gentle green eyes looking down at me. He smiles softly at me, making all the fear I had felt only seconds ago melt away. I know that if he is still smiling at me then everything will be just fine.

"Let's go Colomba, we shouldn't be late for class. We've got better things to do than associate with a pathetic little creep like him." Anthony uses his thumb to point at Luis as if he couldn't hear us. From the corner of my eye, I watch as Luis takes a step back in shock at hearing Anthony talk about him like that. Luis looks back down at me with pleading eyes, as if begging me to stand up for him against Anthony, begging me to not believe in what Anthony is saying, to not believe that he is a terrible, pathetic person. I watch his heart break as I smile up at Anthony, knowing that Anthony is telling me the truth. After everything that Luis has done, there's no way that I could think of him as anything less than pathetic, horrible, idiotic, and just plain evil. After what he has done, he has run out of excuses. I forgave him once for what he did before as the Crow, I won't do it again. I shouldn't have forgiven him at all after all he put me through ever since we got into high school, but I can't change the past. I can only try to not be so stupid in the future. I can only try to not be so kind to people who don't deserve it.

"You're right, Anthony. We do have better things to do than that." Anthony keeps his arm around me as the two of us make our way down the hall. Around me, I can see other girls looking at me with pure jealousy when they notice Anthony's arm around me. They whisper to their friends, and I can hear scraps of what they are saying. They are saying that they wish they could be me, having a guy like Anthony wrapping his arm around them. They all think that we are dating now. Are we dating? Glancing up at Anthony, I suddenly realize that we kinda are dating. I mean, we hang out all the time, I'm letting him wrap his arm around me without a second thought about it and I'm enjoying it, and now that I have seen who Luis really is, he is the friend I trust the most. What more could you want in a relationship?

I don't think those girls would want to be me though if they knew what else is going through my mind and heart right now. Anthony and I walk right past Luis, and even though I try my best to not look at him, I can still feel the pain and misery coming off of him. Even though I know what he truly is and what he has done, I still can't stop a wave of pity coming over me. I know I should hate him, but I still feel so much pity for him, I shouldn't be feeling anything like that for him. What is wrong with me?

Anthony must have realized how I feel since he stops us right as we enter my first class, gently holding my hands in his. Looking deeply into my eyes, he smiles softly at me, making my heart pound in my chest.

"Don't worry, Darling. I will always be here to

protect you from him, with or without the costume." He gently embraces me, keeping me close to his chest. I close my eyes, feeling so comforted by his warmth and hearing his strong heartbeat, knowing that he is telling me the truth. I don't have to be afraid; I will not need to go against Luis on my own. I will always have him and that brings me more comfort than anything else in the world right now.

He releases me from his embrace, our hands finding each others, and holding them tightly, never wanting to let go. As we do this, I can still feel Luis watching us from behind, his gaze burning a hole in the back of my head. I don't turn around to look at him though. After what he has done, he is not worthy of my attention.

Anthony gives me a little kiss on my forehead as he tells me that he will meet with me right outside my class as soon as it is done before he rushes off to his class before the next bell rings. With him gone, there is now only me and Luis. I'm standing in my classroom while he is still in the exact same spot he was before. The guy hasn't moved an inch even though he's about to be late for class, but it doesn't really look like he cares about that at all. The only thing on his mind seems to be me.

Luis is just staring at me with his dark eyes, looking at me as if I have just hurt him more than anyone else has in his entire life. In his eyes, I can see how betrayed he feels. I don't know why he feels that way though when he was the one who did all these horrible things. I look away from his gaze and head into the classroom as the final bell rings, leaving Luis alone in the hall, probably to receive a detention for being late.

I sit at my desk, trying to forget about Luis and everything that has been going on so that I can focus on the teacher, but the world doesn't seem to want to let me have any sort of peace. Somewhere behind me, I hear two girls whispering about how they think Anthony and I are dating now. One of them states something though that makes my blood turn to ice.

"It's a bit weird that she's dating Anthony, I always thought she was dating Luis, I mean, they're always hanging out together." The other girl just chuckles at that.

"Yeah, he wishes they were dating, did you see how he looked at them when they walked past him. I swear, he looked like he was ready to die right then and there." I do my best to focus just on the teacher again, but now my thoughts are completely filled with the look of betrayal on Luis's face. My heart aches as everything feels like it is crumbling around me.

A ray of hope comes through the darkness though when I remember Anthony. I am not alone like I have been almost my entire time as Silver Dove, I can lean on him. I know that no matter what happens with Luis, I have Anthony on my side. A smile returns to my face as I focus on the teacher, ready to let my thoughts go somewhere else so that I can start to move on from this betrayal.

Don't miss the previous books in The Adventures of Silver Dove series. Check them out at elizascalia.com.

Eliza Scalia has a master's degree in Clinical

Mental Health from Troy University. She enjoys reading, writing, and needlework. Eliza has been writing since she was in middle school and has self-published the Death's Assistant series for young adults. She lives with her husband Paul and her dog Lady.